PAUL TEMPLE

Francis Henry Durbridge ~~was born in Hull, Yorkshire,~~ in 1912 and was educated at Bradford Grammar School. He was encouraged at an early age to write by his English teacher and went on to read English at Birmingham University. At the age of twenty-one he sold a play to the BBC and continued to write following his graduation whilst working as a stockbroker's clerk.

In 1938, he created the character Paul Temple, a crime novelist and detective. Many others followed and they were hugely successful until the last of the series was completed in 1968. In 1969, the Paul Temple series was adapted for television; and four of the adventures prior to this had been adapted for cinema, albeit with less success than radio and TV. Francis Durbridge also wrote for the stage and continued doing so up until 1991, when *Sweet Revenge* was completed. Additionally, he wrote over twenty other well-received novels, most of which were on the general subject of crime. The last, *Fatal Encounter*, was published after his death in 1998.

Also in this series

FRANCIS DURBRIDGE

Paul Temple:
East of Algiers

COLLINS
CRIME
CLUB

COLLINS CRIME CLUB

An imprint of HarperCollins*Publishers*
1 London Bridge Street
London SE1 9GF
www.harpercollins.co.uk

This paperback edition 2015

First published in Great Britain by
Hodder & Stoughton 1959

Copyright © Francis Durbridge 1959

Francis Durbridge has asserted his right under the Copyright,
Designs and Patents Act, 1988 to be identified as the author of this work

A catalogue record for this book is
available from the British Library

ISBN 978-0-00-812566-0

Set in Sabon by Born Group using Atomik ePublisher from Easypress

Printed by RR Donnelley at Glasgow, UK

MIX
Paper from
responsible sources
FSC™ C007454

Chapter One

'*Pardon, monsieur*. This chair – it is occupied?'

'Yes. I am afraid it is. I am keeping it for a lady.'

For the tenth time a disappointed Frenchman turned away as I laid my hand possessively on the seat of the chair I was keeping for Steve. It was *l'heure de l'apéritif*, and the tables of all the cafés up and down the Champs–Élysées were filled. The nine gentlemen whom I had already prevented from sitting in Steve's chair found places elsewhere and were now regarding me with a certain amount of suspicion. I could tell from their expressions that they were beginning to think that my long-awaited wife was a figment of the imagination. Steve herself had assured me that she would have ample time to finish her shopping by twelve o'clock. We had made our rendezvous for midday at Fouquet's, half-way up the Champs-Elysees, and it was now twenty to one.

Luckily the morning was a glorious one, and the time was passing very pleasantly. The Arc de Triomphe stood out in its crisp greyness against a blue sky and the sun was warm enough to make most people decide to sit at the tables set out on the pavement rather than seek the shade and seclusion of the bar and brasserie inside. The show in front of me was as good as a Music Hall. The Parisian girls in their spring dresses were well aware of the male eyes focused on them as they walked with self-conscious elegance down the broad pavement. Every now and then a sleek car rolled to a halt, its wheels touching the edge of the pavement, and disgorged its passengers into one of the cafés. Further away, on the roadway proper, cars were racing six deep down the hill. Every time the traffic lights changed to red, their tyres shrilled as the brakes were mercilessly applied. A minute later, when the signal changed to green, every engine whined in misery as each driver tried to win the race to the next intersection.

I was just ordering a second Martini when one of the new small Dauphine taxis drew up in front of me. The driver opened his door, and I recognized the long, slim leg that felt its way down to the pavement. I was unable to see its owner because of the mass of parcels and boxes which she was trying to manoeuvre through the narrow door. With the true Parisian's instinct to help a pretty woman, the taxi-driver had bustled out of his seat, and he now took charge of the two largest boxes. I think he was a little disappointed when Steve led him towards me and explained that I would pay his fare.

'I haven't a sou left, but I've found some of the most wonderful bargains. Really there's nowhere in the world like the Rue St. Honoré. Darling, this is Judy Wincott. She's going to join us for a cocktail.'

I suppose I had seen the girl follow Steve out of the taxi with the corner of my eye, but the business with the driver and the fare and the parcels and the general impact of Steve's arrival had diverted my attention from her. I turned to shake hands. She was a smallish girl of about twenty-one. She could have been described as good-looking, for her features

2

followed the pattern which is generally approved by film periodicals and fashion magazines, but I somehow could not find her very attractive. There was a suggestion of aggressiveness, or perhaps efficiency, which made me write her off as not quite my type. I don't mind women being efficient, but I don't think it ought to show.

'Oh, Mr. Temple,' she said as I shepherded my two charges through the maze of tables, 'I hope you don't mind my jumping at the chance of meeting you. Is it really true that your books are based on actual cases you've been involved in?'

'Yes, as a matter of fact it is. Do sit down. I'll try and get us another chair.'

Steve had sat down and was disposing her purchases round her feet. I was doling out notes to the taxi-driver with one hand and signalling to the waiter to bring a third chair with the other.

The girl was still looking at me as if she expected I might utter some Confucian epigram.

'It's amazing to think such things actually do happen,' she said. There was a slight but unmistakable American intonation in her rather high voice.

'What you read in the books is really not so extraordinary. My trouble is I can't write about the most astonishing cases. No one would believe me if I did.'

'Oh, I think you should,' Judy Wincott said with a dazzling smile. '*I* would believe you at any rate.'

The waiter produced a chair from somewhere inside the sleeve of his jacket and by judicious squeezing and elbow prodding we were soon all three ensconced around the small table.

'Miss Wincott was very kind,' Steve explained when I had ordered drinks. 'I would never have found the kind of shoes I wanted if she had not told me about Chico's.'

3

'You know Paris well, Miss Wincott?'

'Not really well, as I should like to. But I do know the principal streets. I've been over two or three times with my father. He come to Europe every year – to hunt out old pictures and antiques and things. He's Benjamin Wincott, the antique dealer, you know. He has a very important shop in New York. Perhaps you've heard of it?'

'No. I'm afraid I haven't.'

'It's very well known,' Miss Wincott resumed her recital cosily. 'Of course he has to travel a great deal. It's no good relying on other people's judgement when *so* much money is involved, is it, and then again Daddy's got such an amazing instinct for what is really good. There aren't many countries in the world he hasn't visited. China, Japan – why we've only just made a little hop across to Tunis to buy a collection of very rare amber pendants. Mrs. Temple tells me you're planning to go on there yourselves in a day or two.'

I caught Steve's eyes for an instant, and her expression confirmed my suspicion that it was more by her own invitation than by Steve's that Miss Wincott had favoured us with the pleasure of her company.

'We may go on there after we've had a look at Algiers,' I admitted.

'To get material for a novel?' Judy Wincott prompted quickly.

'That's the main idea.'

The waiter set the three glasses down expertly, each in front of its proper owner. The American girl had ordered a champagne cocktail. I watched her hand close round the stem and suppressed the beginnings of a shudder. Her nails had been allowed to grow a quarter of an inch beyond the ends of her fingers, filed to a point and carefully enamelled a glistening blood-red colour. She took a sip of her drink and gave a quiet laugh, as if she were remembering some good but private joke.

'I certainly had a good time in Tunis. Talk about champagne! I wonder if you'll meet a boy I got to know quite well, even during the short time we were there. His name's David Foster; he works for Trans-Africa Petroleum.'

She gazed at me enquiringly. Not being a seer I could not tell her whether I was likely to meet Mr. Foster of Trans–Africa Petroleum or not. What I really wanted to do was have a chance to talk to Steve and find out what on earth she had in that mountain of parcels.

I muttered: 'Well, Tunis is a pretty big city, I remember hearing.'

'You're dead right,' Miss Wincott agreed reminiscently. 'David and I certainly turned it inside out that last night. The funniest thing happened . . .'

This Judy Wincott was clearly one of those non-stop expresses. Here we were on a sunny spring morning in the most civilized city in the world, condemned to listen to the egotistical babblings of a spoilt child. I took a long pull at my Martini, but it tasted bitter.

'You'll never believe this,' she forged on. 'When we ended up at my hotel somewhere around dawn, David found he had lost his glasses. He was so high he hadn't noticed till then. Well, we searched everywhere. He still hadn't found them when Daddy and I left for Paris that afternoon. And do you know where they turned up?'

Judy Wincott turned enquiringly first to Steve and then to me. Neither of us knew the answer.

'You tell us,' I suggested.

'The customs man at Orly airport found them in my evening handbag when he searched my case.'

Steve and I snickered politely. Miss Wincott laughed richly and then suddenly stopped. She had had an inspiration.

'Say, this is rather a lucky coincidence. Your going on to Tunis, I mean. You could take David's glasses back, couldn't you? I hope you don't mind my asking.'

'Well, I suppose we could, though I think they'd get there much quicker if you sent them by ordinary mail. We don't expect to be there 'till Thursday.'

'No, I can't do that. David's cable said on no account to send them by ordinary mail. They'd be sure to get broken or lost. Poor lamb, he's absolutely stricken without them.'

I suppose it was the vision of a distant but stricken lamb that softened my heart. Steve shot me a glance which I interpreted as meaning: 'Do the decent thing. Don't let the nation down.' So in a moment of weakness I consented.

'That's swell,' Miss Wincott said, and polished off her champagne cocktail. 'Now it's just a question of how to get the spectacles to you. What hotel are you staying at?'

'We're not at a hotel this time,' Steve explained. 'Some friends of ours have a flat just round the corner in the Avenue Georges V, and they've lent it to us for a day or two. We'll be in this evening. Why not come round about seven and have a drink with us? It's number eighty-nine.'

'Oh, no.' Now that she had what she wanted Miss Wincott was prepared to play shy. 'You've seen enough of me already. I'll only pop in for a tiny moment.'

I noticed with relief that she was gathering up her gloves and preparing to leave us. Lest she should change her mind I stood up and made way for her to pass by. Her farewells were hasty but effusive. We watched her weave her way through the pedestrians on the pavement and hail a passing cab with an imperious stab of her forefinger. She waved back to us as she was borne down the street towards the whirlpool of vehicles in the Place de la Concorde.

'You do pick up some odd friends,' I reproached Steve.

'I couldn't do less than ask her to join us. I was absolutely floundering in the Galeries Lafayette when she rescued me. She spent a whole hour showing me where the best shops were. Then when I told her who I was she seemed pathetically anxious to meet you.'

'I didn't think there was anything very pathetic about Miss Wincott. I would say that everything she does is aimed somehow to promote her own interests.'

'Well,' Steve said, 'I think it shows a nice side of her nature to be so anxious to get that poor man's glasses back to him.'

'I suppose it's possible,' I admitted against my better judgement. 'Drink up, Steve. We're supposed to be meeting the de Chatelets at one, and we shall have to dump your parcels at the flat before then.'

We lunched well but not wisely at the de Chatelets', and then went to see the Exhibition of pictures at the Orangerie. It was almost seven when we got back to the flat in the Avenue Georges V. I had quite forgotten about Judy Wincott, and was sousing my head in cold water when the door bell rang. I combed my hair hurriedly and went to open it.

'Ah,' I said when I saw who it was. 'Come on in. We're just going to have a drink.'

Judy Wincott was flushed and panting, as if she had run all the way up to the fourth floor. She was wearing the same clothes as before lunch and did not look as if she had even taken time to do her face up.

'I mustn't stay,' she said breathlessly. 'Daddy and I are dining at the Embassy and I have a taxi waiting. There are the glasses. David's address is inside the case. I sent him a cable to say you'd be arriving on Thursday, and asked him to meet the Algiers plane.'

She had already gone when Steve came through the double doors that led into the hall, dressed in one of the creations she had bought that morning.

'Has she gone already?'

'Dinner at the Embassy and a carriage waiting without,' I explained, looking down at the spectacles case.

The case was a plain leather one bearing no maker's name. When I opened it a folded sheet of paper jumped up. It bore the heading of the Hotel Bedford in Paris, and a brief message in flowing characters:

David Foster,
c/o Trans-Africa Petroleum, Tunis.
from Judy. 'In Memoriam.'

The spectacles were what is known as the Library style. They were made of very strong and thick tortoiseshell with broad side-pieces which folded protectively over the lenses.

I put them on the bridge of my nose and immediately almost fell over. The lenses were strong and thick and my vision seemed to be twisted into a knot. I took them off hastily and found Steve convulsed with laughter.

'You really ought to wear glasses, Paul,' she said illogically. 'They make you look so learned.'

'This chap Foster must be very near-sighted. No wonder he's hollering for his specs. He must be almost blind without them.'

Steve and I travelled on the afternoon plane to Nice next day. It would have been possible to fly direct to Algiers, but Steve finds that long periods at high altitudes tend to make her head ache. Besides, we both have a particular weakness for the Côte d'Azur and are glad of any excuse to spend a day or two there.

We had booked rooms at a hotel where we had stayed before, just a little way along the Promenade des Anglais from the Negresco. It is a small but very luxurious place and the service is usually impeccable. That afternoon, however, several guests had arrived at the same time, and the reception clerk was in a flat spin. One of the uniformed *chasseurs* accompanied us and our luggage up to the first floor. Even before we turned into the corridor where our room was we could hear the metallic clatter of a key being turned vainly in a lock. Another *chasseur* with a very English-looking guest in tow was trying to open the door of number twelve, the room next to ours. A moment later our own *chasseur* was twisting his key in the lock, rattling the handle and generally behaving like a bad case of claustrophobia.

Suddenly the English-looking guest pushed his *chasseur* aside, took the key out of the door of number twelve, marched up to number thirteen, pushed the second *chasseur* to one side and exchanged the keys. He turned the key and immediately our door swung open. He spun on his heel and directed a suspicious nod at us.

'Pardong, Mushoor,' he said in terrible French. '*Vous avez mon clef.*'

'Not my fault,' I answered in English. 'The desk clerk had his wires crossed.'

The other man started; then his face expressed relief and returning faith.

'English, are you? Well, that's something. For a moment I thought someone was trying to play a trick on us, and Sam Leyland doesn't like that kind of thing.'

Lancashire and proud of it. His voice was powerful and resonant, his dress equally so. He wore a grey check suit which must have been tailored to accommodate the bulge of his stomach. His shoes were rather on the yellow side, but very shiny and amazingly small by comparison with his enormous but top-heavy body. He sported a silk tie with a picture of a ballet dancer on the swelling part, and a fading rose in his button-hole. His face was red and washed-looking; the dome of his head glistened and was innocent of hair. His nose had been broken, perhaps during some encounter with a lamp-post or a business associate. I put him down as one of that breed of Company Directors who by mysterious means make enough money to travel abroad and carry the Union Jack into the Casinos of furthermost Europe. Still, I could not help rather liking him, though I would not have trusted him to time my egg boiling.

'I don't think it was done on purpose,' I reassured him. 'They're usually pretty good here.'

'They'd better be,' the Lancashire man said. 'Their prices are steep enough, and if there is one man who's going to see value for money that's Sam Leyland.'

He was beginning to look angry again, so when Steve began to retreat into our room I followed her.

'Who's this Sam Leyland he was talking about?' she asked me when the door was shut. 'He sounds simply terrifying.'

'Don't be an ass. That was Sam Leyland himself.'

We were destined to encounter Sam later that evening. We were returning from a particularly good dinner at *La Bonne Auberge* soon after ten-thirty. The lift was taking someone up to the top floor, so we decided it would not kill us to use the stairs, though the idea was abhorrent to the night porter, so much so that he almost used physical force to prevent us.

There was no mistaking the voice which we could hear upraised in anger, and when we came round the corner we were not surprised to see Sam Leyland, still with his hat on his head, standing over a terrorized chamber-maid and raising all hell with her. He had found some neutral language, half-way between French and English, which was utterly incomprehensible to anyone else.

When we appeared he shrugged his shoulders and turned away from the chamber-maid in disgust. The demoralized girl seized her chance to scuttle down the corridor and bolt herself into a small room with her brooms and pails.

'I knew there was some monkey business going on here,' Sam thundered as he advanced threateningly on us. 'And someone's going to pay for it or my name isn't Sam Leyland.'

'What's the trouble? Have they switched keys on you again?'

Sam's eyes were rather like an angry porker's, small and fierce, but uncomprehending. He seemed about to speak, but words failed him and he expelled a long breath.

'Come and take a look at this.'

He led the way towards the door of his room. It was open and the key was still on the outside of the lock. The decorative scheme was the same as ours; faint lilac walls, deep blue curtains, black fitted carpet and modern furniture in very light-coloured natural wood. The only real difference was that Sam's room contained a single bed instead of a double and was in a state of unimaginable disorder.

'By Timothy, what a mess! No mistaking the fact that you've had a visitor.'

Sam's answer was a low growl. It was easy to sympathize with his rage. Every drawer had been wrenched open and its contents scattered on the floor, the bedclothes had been torn

11

off and the edges of the mattress ripped open. The pillows had been disembowelled and feathers were everywhere. Sam's cases had been opened and the linings cut loose. Even his shaving set in its leather case had been torn apart and the case ripped up. The general impression of violence and desperation was frightening.

'How simply awful!' Steve exclaimed. 'It must have been a thief. Did you leave anything valuable here?'

For the first time an expression of pleasure flickered across the burly man's face. He patted the bulge of his wallet pocket and nodded wisely at Steve.

'My valuables are all tucked safely away in here. Sam Leyland doesn't believe in taking chances. The best this scallywag is likely to have got away with is a pair of Woolworth's cuff links. It's the mess he's made that annoys me. Well, the hotel staff will just have to find another room for me.'

I felt Steve's fingers suddenly tighten on my arm.

'Paul! The diamond brooch you gave me for my birthday. I left it in the drawer of my dressing-table.'

It was with an absolute conviction that I would find our own room in the same state of disorder that I fumbled the key into the lock and felt for the light switch. The room sprang into relief as the indirect lighting above the wall fluting flooded the ceiling. I heard Steve's sigh of relief when she saw that our room appeared to be just as we had left it. The telephone was ringing, but she ignored it and pushed past me to go towards the dressing-table. I saw her open the drawer, feel around inside, and then hold up the glittering brooch. She was smiling with relief.

'I'm glad he didn't find this.'

'Steve!' I remonstrated. 'How many times have I warned you not to leave valuables in hotel bedrooms?'

'I didn't mean to, darling. If you hadn't kept telling me to hurry up I would never have forgotten it.'

There is no answer to that sort of remark, so I crossed the room, sat on the edge of the bed and picked up the telephone receiver.

'Hello. Temple here.'

'*Monsieur* Temple? I am so sorry to disturb you, *monsieur*, but a police inspector is here and he wishes to speak with you immediately.'

It was the voice of the night-duty clerk at the reception desk.

'Does he say what it is about?' I asked. I was thinking that if they were already on to the hotel thief the police in this part of the world were pretty fast movers.

'No, *monsieur*. He says it is very urgent and he must see you at once.'

I took time to light a cigarette before going down the stairs again. When I reached the foyer I saw the desk clerk nod to a man who was sitting in one of the arm-chairs. He rose at once and came forward to meet me.

Being accustomed to working with the officers of Scotland Yard I was prepared for something rather different. To begin with, this man's size would have prevented him from entering our Police Force. He was too small, perhaps not more than five foot five. He was dark and concentrated, very neat in his appearance and turn-out, with black hair brushed smoothly back, slick collar and shirt cuffs, well-cleaned shoes. His head seemed big by comparison with his body and his eyes extraordinarily keen. He looked more like a musician than a policeman.

'Mr. Temple?' he asked, and I could tell at once that he was going to speak good English.

'Yes.'

13

He perfunctorily showed me a little wallet. I caught a glimpse of his photograph behind a cellophane slip and a flash of the red, blue and white of official France.

'*Inspecteur* Mirabel, of the *Police Judiciaire*. I would like to speak a few words with you in private. I think this room is empty.'

He motioned me into a small room which was only used by those of the hotel's clientele who insisted on coming downstairs to breakfast. The chairs were all hard and upright, and when we sat down one on either side of a bare table, the whole situation seemed very official and unfriendly. Mirabel's manner and tone of voice kept it that way. He opened a small notebook, but did not glance down at it. His eyes were fixed gravely on me.

'Mr. Temple, it is correct that you came here to-day by the 2.20 airplane from Paris?'

'Yes.'

'And before that you were staying at number 89 Avenue Georges V?'

'That is right. Some friends of ours lent us their flat for several days.'

'Were you visited there by a Miss Wincott?'

'Yes,' I said, surprised at the unexpected question. 'Only very briefly. She came to deliver a package and was not in the flat for more than two minutes.'

To myself I was thinking that the instinctive antagonism I had felt towards Judy Wincott had been justified. She was bringing trouble.

'Did you know Miss Wincott well? Please tell me what your relations with her were.'

'My relations were very casual. I had only met her that day. She was rather kind to my wife in Paris yesterday morning, and she invited her to join us for an *apéritif*.'

'That was last night?'

'No. That was before lunch. It was then arranged that she would call on us at the flat about seven that evening—'

'And she did so? Can you remember the exact time?'

'Yes. I think I can. My wife and I got back at seven and she arrived about five minutes later.'

Mirabel made a quick note. I was becoming curious as to how Judy Wincott had aroused the interest of the police, but decided that it was better not to ask any questions just yet.

'Did she give you any address?' Mirabel continued.

'She was staying at the Hotel Bedford, I believe – with her father.'

'Her father?'

Mirabel had looked up in surprise.

'He's Benjamin Wincott, an antique dealer from New York. The American Embassy can tell you more about him than I can. According to Miss Wincott they were dining there last night.'

Mirabel gazed at me for a moment and a little smile touched the corner of his mouth.

'You mentioned a package, Mr. Temple. Please tell me what this was.'

'Oh, it was just a pair of spectacles she asked me to deliver to a friend of hers in Tunis.'

Mirabel's eyebrows rose. I went on to give him a résumé of the tale Judy Wincott had told me.

When I had finished he said: 'I should like to see these spectacles. Would you show them to me, please?'

'Certainly. I have them here.'

I took the case from my breast pocket and handed it over to Mirabel. He extracted the spectacles and turned them over slowly in his long and sensitive fingers. He smoothed the sheet of Hotel Bedford notepaper on the table. I saw his brows furrow. He balanced the case in his hand as if assessing its weight.

'I should like to take these to my headquarters and have them examined by an expert,' he said. 'You do not object?'

'Not at all,' I said. 'You will allow me to have them back? I feel under some obligation—'

'I will give you a receipt,' Mirabel said stiffly. 'Unless there is any reason to the contrary these glasses will be returned to you in the morning.'

'Thank you. May I ask—? Is Miss Wincott in some sort of trouble?'

Mirabel's deep eyes focused on me again and his expression was whimsical.

'I do not think you would say that she was in trouble. Her body was found by the concierge this afternoon in one of the rubbish bins behind your block of flats. She had been shot in the back. The police doctor's estimate of the time of death coincides with your account of the time she left you.'

I didn't say anything. I knew Mirabel was studying me as my thoughts flew back to Fouquet's and the girl who had so exasperated me when she had sat beside me the day before. Murderers themselves usually make sense. It is the victims they choose that somehow startle and shock one. I could have imagined Judy Wincott being smacked by an exasperated suitor, being socially ostracized, even arrested for drunkenness – but not murdered.

'You are surprised?' Mirabel murmured.

'What do you think? She left me at seven last night to join her father and dine at the American Embassy. Does it seem natural that her body should be found to-day in a refuse bin? Have you any ideas as to who did it, or why?'

16

Mirabel shook his head.

'The assassin left no trace. It has taken us until now to find out who it was she was visiting last night and why.'

'Surely her father notified the police when she failed to turn up last night? And I'm surprised her taxi-driver didn't start looking for his fare!'

Again that little smile moved at the side of Mirabel's mouth. I began to feel that I was the object of his amusement.

'We have checked on all foreigners in Paris hotels at the moment. There is no Benjamin Wincott and he is certainly not known to the American Embassy.'

'Have you tried the Bedford Hotel?'

'We have checked at all the big hotels. No one of that name is registered at any recognized hotel.'

Steve and I talked for a long time after we had gone to bed. She was very distressed at the thought that within a few minutes of leaving us Judy Wincott had been attacked and killed.

'One somehow feels that one should have been able to do something to avoid it, Paul. The motive must have been robbery, don't you think?'

'Maybe. Though I should have thought a thief would have been more likely to use a cosh or a razor.'

I felt Steve shiver.

'I'm glad I have you beside me. There seems to be such a lot of crime on the Continent. First the business in the room next door and now the news of this murder.'

At last we put our light out and went to sleep.

Almost at once it seemed that Steve was gently shaking my shoulder. I opened my eyes, saw the pattern of light cast by the moonlight on the wall opposite our bed, and for a moment had to grope in my mind to realize where we were.

'Paul, listen!' Steve's words came in an alarming stage whisper. 'There's something very funny happening in the next room.'

I sat up quickly in bed and listened. It was a curious slithering, bumping noise as if a man were half carrying, half dragging a heavy weight. Through the wall it seemed that I could hear his grunts and heavy breathing. Then there came an especially loud thud against the dividing wall, a series of thumps and the sound of a door closing.

'It's Sam Leyland's room,' Steve said. 'I thought he had moved somewhere else.'

We sat there listening in the dark. The noise had stopped and there was an ominous silence on the other side of the wall.

Beside me I heard a click, and Steve's bedside light flooded the room. I already had one foot out of bed and was reaching for my dressing-gown.

'Something damned fishy is going on. I'm going to have a look and see if he's all right.'

'Then I'm coming too,' Steve said firmly, and slipped out of bed.

We moved out into the corridor so fast that we cannoned into the young man who was at that moment passing our door. He too was wearing a dressing-gown and had apparently been roused from sleep just as we had.

'Sorry,' I said, and then remembering that we were in France I changed it to: *'Pardon.'*

'It's all right,' the young man smiled. 'I'm English too. My room's on the floor below, and I came up to see what all the commotion was about. But if it's only you two having a row . . .'

He was good-looking in a matinee idol sort of way, with side-whiskers just a shade on the long side and a frieze of early morning stubble round his chin. He was tall and well-made, and a dressing-gown of sheer, sky-blue silk was knotted round his middle. His voice was well educated and nicely pitched, his manner of speaking lazy and slow. But his eyes, as they appraised Steve, were obviously missing nothing.

'It wasn't us,' Steve said quickly. 'I was woken up by it, and my husband was just going to investigate. It came from in here.'

She pointed to the door of number twelve. The young man turned back and advanced towards the door. He gave a tentative knock; there was no answer.

'Perhaps we should break in,' he suggested unenthusiastically.

Out of the corner of my eye I saw Steve stoop suddenly and pick something off the floor.

I said: 'Try the handle first.'

The young man turned the handle and pushed. The door swung open into the pitch-dark room. The bulb in the corridor behind us sent a rectangle of light across the floor in which our two shadows loomed like elongated monsters. Someone had pulled the curtains in that room tight shut and the light behind us only served to accentuate the blackness of the rest of the room. We stood there for a moment, tense, as if expecting some nameless horror to burst out at us. Then the young man put a hand up and snapped on the light.

The room was still in a state of chaos, though all Sam Leyland's things had been collected and moved. The only difference was that the curtains were drawn, which they had not been before, and the doors of the big built-in cupboard on the wall adjoining our room were closed. I thought I

19

could see an impression on the bed where a recumbent body might have lain.

'Nobody here,' the young man said. 'But what an extraordinary mess! I think we'd better let the management know.'

I said: 'Hold on a moment.'

I was remembering the thump on the wall which had brought us out of bed. It must have had something to do with that cupboard. I crossed the room, turned the small key in the lock and opened the door. Behind me I heard Steve gasp and the young man utter an exclamation.

The body was lying on the floor of the cupboard, where it had been bundled hastily and unceremoniously. It was that of a girl, and she was wearing clothes which I recognized. Her legs were free, but her wrists were tied with a strip of cloth and a gag was still in her mouth. I lifted her face for a moment before letting it fall back on her chest. Her body was still warm, but there could be no life behind those eyes. My guess was that she had been forcibly brought to that room and then smothered with the pillow which still lay on the bed. Not a very pretty crime.

'Don't look, Steve,' I said, and stood up to shield her from the sight. But Steve had already seen enough and was twisting away in horror. I closed the cupboard door and met the eyes of the young man. He was standing like a statue, trembling violently, every drop of colour drained from his face.

'You'd better let them know downstairs about this,' I told him. 'I'll stay here and look after my wife.'

He seemed glad to go, and vanished without a word. Steve, whose nerves have become harder than those of most women, had pulled herself together quickly.

'Paul!' she said in a low voice. 'You saw who it was. I couldn't mistake that hair and those clothes. It was Judy Wincott!'

I didn't answer. A movement of the curtains had caught my eye, and I was very conscious of the fact that we had come into the room within a minute or so of the murderer completing his work. I pushed Steve back, stepped over to the curtains, and with a quick movement pulled them aside.

In front of me the open windows gaped out on to the night, and the faint sea breeze which had stirred the curtains fanned my face. The greeny light of the street lamps brought the dark walls and gables into ghostly relief. Down below a street cleaner was hosing the pavement and swishing the debris down the gutters with a long brush. From somewhere indeterminate came the smell of tomorrow's bread baking.

I turned back to Steve.

'This must be the way he went. We can't have missed him by much. He may even have been watching us when we opened that cupboard.'

Chapter Two

THERE was little sleep in store for Steve and me that night. At my suggestion Mirabel was summoned and a cold-looking dawn was lightening the sky before we had made our statements and been given permission to withdraw.

We were awakened by a buzz on the house telephone at ten o'clock. A quarter of an hour later our *petit déjeuner* was brought up on a nice big tray. We had barely finished our coffee and croissants when the 'phone buzzed once more. Mirabel was in the hall below and wanted to see me again.

'I'm just going to have a bath,' Steve said. 'You can tell him to come up here.'

'I'm afraid I'm not dressed yet,' I told the telephone. 'Would you mind coming up to room number thirteen? Or if you'd rather I'll get dressed and be down in about ten minutes.'

Mirabel decided to come up. Within a minute he was at the door. He had found time to shave and change his collar. Spick and span as he was, he looked very out of place in our chaotic bedroom. I pulled him up a chair and offered him a cigarette, which he refused. I thought, however, that his manner was more friendly than the previous night.

22

'Are you any further on?' I asked, trying to show the right amount of polite interest.

'I have had time to communicate with our English colleagues and obtain some information about you, Mr. Temple. They tell me that though you have a gift for attracting trouble towards you, you are not usually the prime cause of it.'

I laughed, imagining Vosper's wording of such a message.

'Then I'm off your list of suspects?'

'I think so,' Mirabel said and smiled. 'You will be interested to hear that we have solved the mystery of the same woman being murdered twice. It now appears that the girl found in the dustbin behind your flat was not Judy Wincott at all, though she was half American too and her name was Diana Simmonds. Our mistake was a natural one, since a letter found in her bag bore the name Judy Wincott and the murdered woman resembled her enough for the concierge to mistake her for the Miss Judy Wincott who had enquired for you the previous evening.'

Mirabel seemed prepared to dismiss the subject at that. I expected him to ask me a great many more questions and there were several that I would like to have put myself. But the Inspector limited himself to feeling in his breast pocket and producing a small object wrapped in tissue paper.

'I am returning the glasses to you as I promised,' he said. 'Without the case, though. Our people soon reduced that to its elemental components.'

'Did you find anything?'

Mirabel shook his head.

'Nothing at all.'

'Did you have the spectacles checked?'

'Yes, of course. There is nothing unusual about them. They are a perfectly ordinary pair of spectacles.'

He unwrapped them from their tissue paper and inspected them casually before handing them across to me.

'Genuine tortoiseshell, too clear to conceal anything. And the lenses – well, there is nothing, is there?'

I took the glasses reluctantly.

'I can't help wondering. All the trouble seemed to begin from the moment these spectacles came into my life . . .'

'You can rest assured, Mr. Temple. If there were anything abnormal about those spectacles our experts would have found out about it.'

The Inspector rose to his feet and pulled his jacket down.

'I am sorry that your holiday has been interrupted in such an unpleasant way, and grateful to you for your co-operation.'

He held out his hand.

'Give my homage to madame, your wife. I hope you will have a pleasant journey to Tunis.'

'We are free to carry on?' I said, still surprised that Mirabel was letting us off so lightly. 'You won't require us to give evidence at the inquest?'

'It will not be necessary,' Mirabel assured me. 'You can continue your journey and Mr. David Foster can recover his spectacles – which I feel he must be missing very badly.'

I had risen to my feet at the same time as Mirabel but I still felt reluctant to let him go.

'Will you forgive me, *Inspecteur*, if I ask you something?'

Mirabel shrugged non-committally, but he waited for my question.

'This woman who was murdered in the Avenue Georges V – do you know who she was?'

'We have found that out,' Mirabel said readily enough. 'She had several names but the one she used the most of the time was Lydia Maresse. She was known to Interpol as an international criminal.'

'Any idea of the motive for her murder?'

'None at all.'

I hesitated for a moment while Mirabel studied me quizzically.

'*Inspecteur* – it surely does not escape you that there must be some connection between the two crimes, since Judy Wincott's handbag was planted on the body found in Paris. Nor can it have failed to strike you as odd that my wife and I should have been so close at hand on each occasion.'

Mirabel raised his eyebrows and studied his immaculate nails.

'These facts had not escaped us, Mr. Temple. But we are satisfied none the less that you had nothing to do with either crime.'

He suddenly smiled, offered me his hand again and turned to the door. It had almost closed on him when his head was poked in again.

'If by any chance I need to contact you again I can always be sure of finding you. Thanks to Interpol we can reach the people who interest us in almost any country in the world.'

Steve and I had half a day to kill. We were again booked for the afternoon flight, this time to Algiers. I felt that what she most wanted was a breath of honest fresh air, as far away from that accursed hotel as possible. Enquiries at the hotel desk revealed that it was quite feasible to hire a small yacht. Sailing is a sport both Steve and I are addicted to and by half-past eleven we were well out from the shore in a neat little dinghy with racy lines.

For an hour we enjoyed the illusion that no inquisitive or prying eyes were watching us. From out at sea Nice, with its long promenade of white buildings, gay sun shades and the hills rising in tiers behind it, looked even more attractive than from land. A number of other craft were out on the water. Several speed-boats were towing water ski-ers at speed across the bay and there were a dozen other yachts of various sizes about. The water was not rough, but there was enough of a breeze to make sailing an energetic job that occupied most of our attention. Every now and then an aircraft taking off from the Nice airport skimmed low over our heads.

The wind was whipping the hair away from Steve's ears, and I could see the colour returning to her pallid cheeks. We had just gone about for the twentieth time and were sitting on the gunwale to counterbalance the dinghy when she pointed to one of the speed-boats which had been cruising in our vicinity for some time.

'He seems very interested in us,' she called to me above the noise of the spray and the water swishing under our bows. 'I think he's watching us through binoculars.'

I glanced at the launch and then turned to laugh at Steve. She is a very attractive woman, but unusually modest, and she can never bring herself to attribute the attention and interest of other gentlemen to the very apparent attractiveness of her person. In the blue trousers and scarlet shirt she was wearing this morning she was likely to be the target for more than one pair of eyes.

A sudden gust of wind made the dinghy tip over dangerously, and we had to lean right back to keep her sails up out of the water. It was quite a tricky moment, and several hectic minutes passed before we had things under control again. Our canvas hid the cruising speedboat from us until I brought the dinghy's head round to work her back to the shore. The noise of wind and water was so high that we had been unable to hear the sound of the engine. Even when I did hear the powerful roar I thought that it was just another aircraft taking off.

Steve's shout switched my attention to our starboard beam.

'Alter course, Paul. He's coming straight for us!'

I looked up and saw the speed-boat no more than twenty yards away. Her engines must have been at full power, for her bows were well clear of the surface. A cliff of water seemed to be sheering away from either side of her steeply sloping sides. Every time she hit a wave the white foam went hissing outwards.

She must have been doing thirty or forty knots. On her present course she must surely ram us.

It was hopeless to shout and attract the attention of the pilot. He wouldn't have heard us, and anyway his bows were riding so high that I doubted whether he could see us.

I slammed the tiller over and ducked as the boom came across. The dinghy yawed. She had lost all momentum and wallowed in a trough of water, a helpless and motionless prey for the oncoming speed-boat. She bore down on us like a swooping hawk.

When she was twenty yards away I shouted to Steve: 'Jump for it!'

Hand in hand we leapt into the sea, as far from the path of the speed-boat as we could. Even as we rose to the surface we heard the crash behind us and the splinter of wood. The big speed-boat had cut the flimsy dinghy clean in two. Next instant a wall of creamy water hit us, filling our eyes and noses, thrusting us deep under the water. All the time I kept Steve's hand clutched in mine.

When we got our heads above water and recovered our breath the hum of the speed-boat was quite distant. A wave lifted me up and I saw his wake disappearing in the direction of Monte Carlo.

The biggest piece of wreckage left was a section of the mast, which had a life-belt attached to it. Dragging Steve, I paddled towards it and we each grabbed hold of one side.

'Well,' Steve remarked to me bitterly, between gasping breaths. 'Do you still maintain that the man in that boat was only interested in my elegant torso?'

As we bobbed aimlessly up and down, the coast seemed to be as far away as the Antipodes. None of the other craft in the neighbourhood had noticed the accident, and there was not enough of our dinghy left to attract attention. Luckily the water was not unbearably cold. I thought we could hold on till darkness at least. During that time someone must surely come near enough to spot us.

In the end it was less than ten minutes before we were found. A rather slow but obviously safe fishing-boat came chugging out straight towards us. As it drew near I began to wonder if there was going to be room on board, since half the population of Nice's old quarter seemed to have thumbed a ride out to watch the rescue.

So many willing helpers reached down to haul us out of the water that our arms were nearly pulled out of their sockets. There were even some especially keen rescuers who would have been only too willing to apply artificial respiration to Steve.

'*Doucement, doucement! Faîtes place pour Madame.*'

The accent was pretty good, but there was still that slight broadness of speech which betrays the Englishman. I looked round and saw the young man who had shared our discovery of Judy Wincott's body. His name, as I knew all too well by now, was Tony Wyse. He seemed to have been accepted by the crew and passengers as the leader of the salvage operations, and in answer to his instructions room was made for us while dry pullovers and jackets were pressed on our soaked bodies.

'It was a bit of luck I saw it all happen,' Wyse told us, as he held his lighter to the cigarettes we had accepted. 'I'm interested in sailing myself, and I was watching your yacht through one of those penny-in-the-slot telescopes they have on the front.'

Steve and I exchanged an amused glance. We had been speculating that morning on the convenience of those same telescopes for gentlemen who are keen on bird watching.

'Did you see what happened?' I asked him. 'I'd like to lay my hands on the owner of that speed-boat. For one thing the dinghy's a total loss and someone will have to pay for her.'

'You needn't worry about that,' Wyse assured me airily. 'They all have pretty comprehensive insurance.'

His day attire was as colourful as his night wear. He sported a pair of fawn flannel trousers which were as inno-cent of wrinkle as of spot, intermesh shoes, one of those Spanish-cut shirts with horizontal stripes and sailor neck, which you wear outside your trousers, and a silk neckerchief tied round his throat – more for beauty than for warmth. 'Killer' was written all over him, but strictly a lady-killer. He was not a man's man.

'He did it on purpose,' Steve stated rather wildly. 'I knew he was watching us in a malice aforethought kind of way. If we hadn't jumped into the sea we would have been killed. I tell you, Paul, it's all because of those confounded—'

'It certainly was a freak accident,' I interrupted quickly, and turned to Wyse. 'How did it seem to you?'

Wyse raised a shoulder elegantly.

'It's hard to say whether he saw your boat or not. But you can't seriously be suggesting that he ran you down on purpose, can you? I mean, you don't even know who it was, do you?'

Wyse's tone was that of an elder soothing the fears of children who have just awakened from a nightmare.

'Then why—' Steve began.

'No, of course not,' I said, and tried to quell Steve's protestations with a wink. 'It was just one of those million to one chances. We're none the less grateful to you for coming so promptly to the rescue. It looks as if we may still catch this afternoon's plane to Algiers.'

'You're flying to Algiers to-day?' Wyse queried. He smiled broadly and his eyes rested comfortably on Steve's face. 'But this is going to be delightful. I shall be on the Algiers plane myself.'

We caught the Algiers plane with only a minute to spare. It had taken me a long time to come to terms with the owner of the dinghy. We were forced to fling our things into the suitcases and bolt our lunch before careering out to the airport in a taxi. The other passengers had already been escorted to the big Air France machine. Luckily there were no customs or immigration formalities to be observed, and a smartly uniformed young woman marched us rapidly out to the aircraft, just before the steps were wheeled away.

Our seats were half-way along the aircraft. At our own request we each had a seat next to the window, and so were sitting opposite to each other. By no means all the available space in the aircraft had been booked, but the seat next to Steve's was occupied by a vision whose age I put at somewhere between twenty-two and twenty-seven. That she was French seemed obvious from the start. She drew her legs demurely aside to let Steve squeeze past and, under the guise of a friendly smile, the two women exchanged a wary, appraising glance.

The contrast between them was very marked. Whereas Steve was dark and did not have recourse to much makeup, this girl was an ash-blonde. Her hair was so immaculately dressed and glistening that I felt certain she must have been to the coiffeur that morning. Her eye-lashes were too long to be all her own, her nails were varnished and her lips were tinted by a faintly mauve lipstick. Yet there was nothing flashy or cheap about her appearance. You felt rather that she was a very lovely woman who took the maximum care to present herself well.

She must have been a novice at air travel, for when the illuminated sign was switched on she fumbled helplessly with her seat belt and got her own straps mixed up with Steve's. Steve showed her how to fasten herself in.

The French girl smiled charmingly and groped in her mind for words.

'Sank you very mush,' she said, and gave a shy laugh.

'Not at all,' Steve said. 'You're not very accustomed to air travel?'

'Please?'

'I said: you have not travelled by air-o-plane much before?'

The French girl shook her head a little, but not so much as to disturb the ash-blonde hair.

'Yes, sometimes already but not since several years.'

The aircraft was turning on the tarmac, preparing to lumber out to the end of the runway. The stewardess, a reassuring smile on her face, was moving up the aisle, asking passengers to put their cigarettes out, making sure their belts were properly fastened. The French girl was leaning forward,

31

looking out of the window rather nervously at the rapidly passing ground. I knew that Steve was trying to keep her mind from the take-off when she resumed the conversation.

'You are staying in Algiers or going further on?'

'I go to Tunis. But of course I must first stop at Algiers and catch the airplane to Tunis the next day.'

'That's what we are doing. We shall be fellow passengers again to-morrow then.'

'Yes. I shall begin to know you very well. I saw you in the hotel last night when the police were questioning all the guests.'

'Oh, you were staying there too, were you?'

'It must have been terribly *désagréable* for you to find that poor girl like that.'

'Yes,' Steve agreed. 'It was.'

'How horrible to think that you were in the very next room while an assassin was committing his crime!'

Now that she was warming to the conversation the French girl's English was improving. She seemed very interested indeed in all the circumstances of Judy Wincott's murder and began to ply Steve with questions.

'Do you believe it was an attempt to make the police believe you and your husband had committed the crime?'

Steve shot me a startled glance.

'Good gracious, I don't think so.'

'But it is a fact that if the other *monsieur* had not been there you would have been in a situation – *très embarassante*.'

'Well, perhaps we would—' Steve began.

'Though myself I think that she was murdered before she was brought to the room next to yours.'

'Oh?' Steve said. 'Then why did the murderer make such a noise about placing her body in the cupboard?'

'Well,' the French girl said thoughtfully. 'He may have wanted that you should do *précisément* that which you did – precipitate yourselves into the room where the body was finding itself.'

The aircraft had reached the end of the runway and the roar of the engines as the pilot tested them precluded further conversation. The stewardess had strapped herself into her own seat at the rear end. After a momentary hush the engines roared again and the machine began to rush over the ground at rapidly increasing speed. The French girl leant her head back against the seat cushion and I saw her throat move as she swallowed. It was the only sign she gave that she was nervous.

In a few moments our wheels were clear, the flight became smooth and the sea was below us, dropping away rapidly as the aircraft banked and turned southwards towards the North African coast. The sign enjoining passengers to desist from smoking went out, and from all around came the clinking of clasps as people released themselves from their safety belts.

As soon as her buckle was undone the French girl picked up her handbag, and her long, shapely fingers groped for a tiny gold cigarette-case. She took a cigarette, placed it carefully in a holder and put it in her mouth. Then she handed the case to Steve, who smiled and accepted one of the Egyptian cigarettes. The French girl felt in her bag again and produced a new container of book matches. The cover was plain blue, stamped in gilt with the initials S.L.

She struck a match and held it for Steve. I saw my wife staring in a very curious way at the book matches. Then she collected herself and puffed at her light.

'You like my matches?' The French girl had also noticed Steve's expression and was smiling. 'These are my initials. Simone Lalange. It is quite charming, is it not?'

I thought Steve's assent a little forced, and I was disappointed in her when she broke off the conversation. I began to wonder if she was feeling air-sick, for her expression had altered and she was watching me in an expectant kind of way.

I leaned across the table.

'Feeling all right, Steve?'

'Yes, thanks. More or less. I could use a brandy to steady my tummy though. We must have eaten that meal in record time.'

'There's a bar in the tail of this machine. Shall we go and have a drink?'

No one else had yet thought of visiting the bar, so we had the little compartment to ourselves.

'Paul!' Steve said excitedly as soon as the steward had moved behind his tiny counter. 'You remember when we were standing outside that bedroom last night – just before we discovered the body?'

'I do. Most emphatically.'

'Well, I noticed something on the floor and picked it up. It was an empty box of book matches.'

'Yes, I noticed you stooping and wondered what you'd dropped. I'd forgotten all about it.'

'So had I. But I distinctly remember now. It had a blue cover with the initials S.L. on it.'

I shot an instinctive glance towards the seats we had just vacated.

'You saw the book matches that French girl had,' Steve pursued. 'They were an exact replica.'

'Did you tell the police about your find? It's rather important.'

'No. I'd forgotten all about it until now. The thing is still in the pocket of my dressing-gown. You know the way a shock drives everything that's happened previously out of your mind?'

'Perhaps it's not so very important,' I reassured her.
'Mademoiselle Lalange may have been shown the room before
it was allotted to Mr. Sam Leyland, or she may have thrown
it away at any time when she was passing by.'

'Maybe,' Steve said doubtfully. 'But did you hear what
she had to say about the murder? She seemed to have more
theories than anyone else.'

'Well, if you really do regard her with suspicion, I suggest
you behave in a more friendly way to her. She's more likely
to open up if you don't give her the cold shoulder.'

'Did I give her the cold shoulder?'

'Yes. You closed up like a clam the moment she'd lit
your cigarette for you. I can't really bring myself to believe
she's mixed up in this, but I think you should cultivate
her. In any case she'd make a very interesting friend for
the family.'

Steve's glance had the glint of a dagger in it.

'I know you think my theories are all very amusing,' she
said. 'But I'm convinced that some very monkey business
is going on, and equally convinced that it has to do with
those spectacles. It was because of them that Judy Wincott
was murdered, and because of them that we were run down
by that launch this morning. Someone is prepared to stop
at nothing to prevent us delivering them to David Foster.'

'Whereas you are not prepared to let anything stop you
doing so?'

'Right first time,' Steve answered belligerently, and her
mouth set in the firm line which indicates that she really
means business.

The aircraft had gained its cruising height now and had
levelled off. I set my drink down on the low bar table and
watched Steve with amusement.

'If the glasses are so vitally important I'm glad you took charge of them, Steve. By the way I suppose you still have them?'

'Of course I have. They're in my handbag.'

She opened her handbag to prove the point to me, and a second later was groping about feverishly among the collection of assorted and mysterious objects she keeps in there. Then she withdrew her hand and closed the bag deliberately.

'They're gone! Someone must have taken them from my bag since we got on the plane. They were there when we showed our tickets. That French girl! I knew she—'

Steve was already rising when I put a hand to stop her. I patted my handkerchief pocket where the glasses were safely reposing.

'I thought it wise to relieve you of the responsibility. Have you forgotten that since we've been married you've lost three of the handbags I gave you?'

Steve looked at me with undisguised repugnance as she rose to her feet.

'You are not fit to command the loyalty of a decent woman,' she said in her most regal tone, and marched out of the bar.

I was not left alone in the bar for long. Either by chance or because he had seen Steve leave, Tony Wyse appeared within a few moments. He greeted me enthusiastically, and after ordering a brandy and soda sat down beside me. He had changed for the journey into a dark grey suit, suède bootees and a striped tie. After the events of the previous night and the rescue operations that morning he was prepared to regard me as a long-lost brother.

'One thing puzzles me about that business last night, Temple. When you opened the cupboard door and disclosed the simply ghastly spectacle of that slaughtered girl, your wife gave vent to a comment which has made me ponder more than somewhat. She seemed to know at once who it was.'

Wyse raised his glass, but he was studying me closely as he put his question.

'Was she a friend of yours?'

'Not exactly a friend. We'd met her briefly in Paris. That's all.'

'In Paris?'

The information seemed to surprise Wyse.

'Yes. It was a chance encounter. She was very kind to my wife and we invited her to have a drink with us.'

'You told the police this?'

'Yes, of course. Did you imagine I was trying to hide something?'

'No, indeed.' Wyse hurriedly took a sip of his brandy and switched on the charm, which just for a moment had worn thin. 'I'm sorry to appear to be so inquisitive, but one can't help wondering about a murder, especially when one stumbles on the victim before she's even cold.'

'I'm afraid I can't enlighten you,' I said.

Wyse seemed prepared to take the hint implied in my tone of voice and changed the subject.

'This is your first trip to French North Africa?'

'Yes, it is.'

'Perhaps I can be of some service to you? I know both Algiers and Tunis pretty well. I would esteem it a privilege if you would permit me to conduct your wife and yourself round some of the curiosities.'

I thought that a whole day of Wyse's roundabout brand of conversation would send me out of my mind.

I said: 'It's very kind of you, but we are hoping to meet friends there. Does your business bring you out here?'

'Yes. I work for Freeman & Bailey – the engineering firm, you know. We have a good deal of business with Trans-Africa Petroleum.'

'Trans-Africa Petroleum? Perhaps you know a slight acquaintance of mine who's in that firm? His name is David Foster.'

'David Foster?' Wyse echoed the words with judicious thoughtfulness. 'No. I can't say I know him. Of course, I'm constantly on the move, so I miss meeting everyone.'

'You are an engineer yourself?'

'No. Not really an engineer. I am in the liaison department, as you might say – I hold a roving brief.'

He smiled broadly, but I felt that where questions were concerned, he did not relish being at the receiving end. He excused himself, signalled to the steward and made his exit.

The bar was becoming fuller, and I decided it was time I made way for someone else. I was already rising when the gentle pressure of a hand on my shoulder stopped me. I looked down at the hand. It was podgy and very white. Little dimples smiled at the backs of the fingers. Beyond snow-white silk cuffs was the black material of a very expensive suit. My eyes travelled upwards till they had taken in the appearance of the man who had sat down beside me.

I disliked him at once. He was too reminiscent of a white slug. That sickly sweet perfume which he exhaled suggested that his own odour must be strong and unpleasant. His eyes were small, his mouth lascivious. He was growing bald on top but allowed his back hair to curl upwards over the back of his collar.

'One moment, please. You are Mr. Temple, are you not?'

He spoke with his mouth offensively close to my face, more in a whisper than in a normal speaking voice.

38

'I am. I don't think I have the pleasure of knowing you.'

'Maybe not,' the plump man said. 'My name is Constantin. Blanys Constantin. You, I think, are Mr. Paul Temple?'

I did not answer. The steward came to enquire what Constantin wanted to drink, but he waved him away impatiently.

'You were in Nice last night, Mr. Temple, staying at the hotel where a girl named Judy Wincott was murdered.'

'Yes,' I agreed. 'The newspapers made a good story of it.'

'Not a complete story. They did not say that you had met Miss Wincott in Paris.'

'Perhaps they did not consider it a very important piece of news.'

'Other people might consider it interesting, though, might they not, Mr. Temple? Especially if they knew the reason for her visit to your flat in the Avenue Georges V.'

The man had edged even closer, and his voice had dropped. As I was at the end of the couch I had no means of escape unless I was prepared to use violence on him.

'You did not tell the police that she had entrusted you with a certain very valuable document, did you, Mr. Temple?'

My anger was beginning to rise, but I continued to keep my voice down.

'I did not tell them so because it would have been quite untrue.'

'Come, come,' Constantin said. 'You and I know better than that.'

'If you want the truth, Miss Wincott simply asked me to return a pair of spectacles to a Mr. David Foster who lives in Tunis – where my wife and I happen to be going.'

Constantin blinked rapidly several times. For a moment he seemed floored, then returned rapidly to the attack.

'You are being made a fool of, Mr. Temple. There is no such person as Mr. David Foster, and those spectacles will only bring difficulties for you.'

'I think it is you who are being a fool, Mr. Constantin. The spectacles are a perfectly ordinary pair – there's nothing mystic or magic about them, and there's no possibility that they are connected in any way with the murder of Miss Wincott.'

'Nevertheless,' Constantin's eyes flickered rapidly round to make sure that no one was taking an interest in our conversation. 'Nevertheless, I will give you a thousand pounds if you will hand those spectacles over to me.'

I began to laugh and shake my head, but Constantin pressed me back into my seat.

'Five thousand pounds,' he said with intensity, and then almost without a pause: 'Ten thousand! Do not think that I cannot pay so much, because I can. You can collect the money as soon as we arrive in Algiers.'

'You are wasting your time,' I said bluntly, and this time I did push him out of my way so that I could get up.

'No,' he called after me quite loudly as I left the bar. 'It is you who are wasting time. I tell you, you will never find your David Foster!'

Chapter Three

BACK IN the main compartment I found that Steve had sacrificed her seat to the French girl. The latter had, however, tired of gazing down at the unchanging sea; her head had fallen back and she was fast asleep, her chest rising and falling with each deep breath. I signalled to Steve, who moved quickly round to sit in the empty seat beside me.

'Your instinct was right. There is some curious significance in those spectacles. I can't think why, but there are people who are prepared to pay big money for them. And when big money is at stake you have an ample motive for murder.'

I told her about my encounter with Constantin and the fabulous offer he had made. Steve nodded, her eyes on the sleeping girl. She took it all in as if it were merely the confirmation of something she had known all along.

'The reason for the murders of those two girls is in your breast pocket,' she said softly. 'I've discovered something interesting too. I've had quite a talk with her.'

She gestured towards the sleeping Simone Lalange.

'She practically told me her life history. Do you know what came out? Her reason for going to Tunis is that she has friends in Trans-Africa Petroleum. It seems an amazing coincidence.'

'Does she know David Foster?'

'I asked her that, but she said she still only knew the names of a few people in the firm.'

We both contemplated the girl in the opposite seat, and I think the same question was in each of our minds. What had she been doing at the door of room number twelve the previous night?

The rest of our flight was uneventful. Neither Constantin nor Wyse came near us again. As far as Simone Lalange was concerned our relations only grew more friendly. She now directed her attention more towards me, unmasking the full battery of her considerable charm. I alone was aware of the double meaning which was creeping into some of Steve's apparently innocent remarks. I was quite relieved when the long North African coast line came into view and we began to lose height for the landing at Maison Blanche.

Air France had booked accommodation for most passengers at the Aletti Hotel, the most modern hotel in Algiers, which stands facing the harbour. When the company bus set us down at the door I noticed that both Tony Wyse and Simone Lalange were also to be at the Aletti. Of Constantin there had been no sign since the aircraft doors had opened. He had either been met by friends or found some private transport of his own.

In view of the disturbances in Algeria the police were insisting on all the regulations with regard to travellers being rigidly observed. The reception clerk asked us to fill in the usual *fiche de voyageur* even before we were shown our rooms. When I handed mine in he glanced at the name and then raised his eyebrows.

'Mr. Temple? There has been a telephone call for you. A gentleman rang up about half an hour ago to ask if you had arrived yet.'

'That's odd,' I said to Steve. 'I don't know anyone in Algiers. Certainly I haven't told anyone I was coming.'

I turned to the clerk: 'Did he give any name?'

'No, *monsieur*. He said he would telephone you again later.'

Our room in the Aletti Hotel was a truly magnificent one, affording us a splendid view of the harbour which had once served as a base for the pirates who had terrorized shipping in the Mediterranean. A big French passenger liner was berthed in the inner harbour within a couple of hundred yards of Algiers' busy streets. Though there was a general feeling of tension in the air, as if everyone was expecting a bomb to explode, there were few visible signs of the violence which was splitting Algeria apart and keeping a whole Army of French troops occupied in the mountains farther south. The pedestrians on the pavements below were an odd mixture of French and Arabs. Many of the latter wore European clothes with perhaps only a fez or their swarthier features to distinguish them, but there were a number of shambling figures in Arab dress. They wore the curious one-piece tweed garment with hood attached which goes by the name of *cachabia*. Often their feet were bare, their features pinched and soiled. They were very different from the romantic notion of the proud Bedouin astride his camel.

'I hope there isn't going to be a revolution while we're here,' Steve remarked as she carefully took her dresses from the travelling case and hung them in the wardrobe. 'I know you'd think it was marvellous material for some book, but I personally don't relish the idea of being knifed in the street. And talking of knifing, Paul, I wish you'd deposit those glasses in some safe place.'

'You don't trust me with them?'

43

'It's not that. If this man Constantin wants them badly enough to offer you ten thousand pounds he may easily make violent attempts to get them from you. You said yourself that when big money is at stake there's an ample motive for murder. Why don't you ask the hotel manager to put the glasses in the safe?'

I went through into the little bathroom to arrange my washing and shaving things on the shelf.

'You can't expect me solemnly to ask the manager of a hotel to put a perfectly ordinary pair of spectacles in his safe. Everyone would think I was dotty. Besides, it would only attract attention.'

'They *can't* just be an ordinary pair of glasses,' Steve objected. 'They must have some special value for this David Foster person.'

'I can't see quite why. The French police are very thorough, and you can be sure they subjected the spectacles to an exhaustive scrutiny.'

I took the spectacles out of my pocket as I went back into the bedroom and placed them on the table in the middle of the room. Steve stood beside me and we both looked down at them. It was hard to imagine anything more homely and prosaic. They reminded me of one of the most kindly and gullible of my masters at school, and I associated them with a smell of pipe tobacco, leather bindings and the cosy sound of a motor-mower on a cricket pitch. Yet since they had come into my hands two girls had been brutally done to death, a crude attempt had been made to drown Steve and me, and a complete stranger had made me an offer of ten thousand pounds.

'I just don't understand your attitude, Paul.' Steve's tone showed that she had mis-read my thoughts. 'You aren't even prepared to take this seriously.'

I turned to her and put my hands on her shoulders.

'I do take this seriously, Steve. I'm quite prepared to believe that there's some sinister, perhaps deadly secret attached to them. But I gave my word to a girl who is now dead that I would deliver them. My object is to do so as quickly as possible and wash my hands of the whole business. Then you and I can carry on with our holiday as planned.'

Steve did not respond to my smile. Her eyes were clouded and there were three little lines across her brow.

'Suppose Constantin is right and you don't succeed in finding David Foster. There may not be any such person.'

'In that case I'll take the glasses back to France and hand them over to the police. All the same I think David Foster exists – though he may well be known by another name. It's even possible that we've met him already.'

'You think he might be Tony Wyse? In that case why does he not ask you outright to hand over his property? But I don't think that theory holds water. I can't believe there's much wrong with Mr. Wyse's eyesight.'

It was significant of our feelings that when the telephone rang my first action was to tuck the glasses safely away in my breast pocket and arrange my handkerchief to cover them. Only when that was done to the satisfaction of both of us did I cross to the bedside table and lift the receiver.

'Who is it?'

'Is that Mr. Temple?'

'Yes. Who's that speaking?'

'It's David Foster here. I understand you have my spectacles. I thought I'd ring up and arrange to collect them from you.'

'Oh, Mr. Foster?' I echoed the name, looking at Steve as I did so. She immediately came and stood with her ear close to the other side of the receiver, straining to catch both sides of the conversation. 'I didn't expect to hear from you till we reached Tunis.'

'Oh. I see. Well I had to come over to Algiers for a few days on business. I had a cable from Judy and she told me you would be coming this way. I thought it would save you further trouble if I relieved you of the glasses right away.'

'Yes,' I said. 'I expect you find life rather complicated without them.'

'Oh?' The voice sounded suspicious. 'How do you mean?'

'Well, I expect it's difficult for you to read and that sort of thing.'

'Oh, yes, of course.' The caller laughed nervously. 'Yes, I keep tripping over things and taking the wrong bus and so on. It's an awful nuisance. Will you be in if I come round right away?'

'Yes. About how long will you be?'

'Oh, not long. I'm at the Villa Negra—' The voice suddenly broke off. I put my hand over the receiver and turned to Steve. 'We seem to have been cut off.'

Steve said: 'It sounded to me more as if he had done just what you have – put his hand over the mouthpiece—'

I held my finger up to silence her. The voice on the telephone was speaking again.

'Are you there?'

'Yes. Still here.'

'I'll call in about twenty minutes. Can you wait for me in the hotel lounge?'

'Yes. Ask the reception clerk and he'll show you where we're sitting.'

'Good. By the way, how is Judy?'

'Judy Wincott? I'm afraid I have some bad news for you, but it had better keep till we meet.'

46

'Bad news?'

'I'm afraid so. See you in about twenty minutes.'

It was twenty-two minutes past seven when I put the receiver down. Steve and I were in the lounge by half-past seven, and had briefed the reception clerk to show our visitor where we were sitting. At half-past eight I checked with the desk for the third time, but no one had asked for Temple.

'Nothing doing,' I told Steve as I joined her again. 'I'm afraid our bird is not going to turn up.'

'I thought there was something fishy about that conversation. Could it have been your friend Constantin?'

'No. I'd have recognized that voice, even on the telephone. Perhaps he's taken the wrong bus again.'

'I suppose there's no way of tracing the call?'

'He did mention the Villa Negra, though it seemed to me that the name slipped out unintentionally. Perhaps the staff behind the reception desk would help us. There are enough of them.'

The chief clerk was distant and doubtful, but when I said I would have to call in the police he changed his tune. Directories were produced, and at the end of ten minutes he beckoned me over and showed me a map of Algiers.

The Villa Negra was a large house overlooking a small private bay to the West of Algiers. It was about a quarter of an hour away by car or taxi.

'Can you get a taxi for us?' I asked the clerk.

'There's no need, *monsieur*. Always there is at least one taxi waiting outside the hotel.'

He snapped his fingers at a *chasseur* who, scenting a tip, rushed forward with alacrity.

'Show *monsieur* to a taxi.'

47

'Dinner?' Steve enquired when I told her that we were going. 'I must say I'm ready for it.'

'Not yet, I'm afraid. First, the Villa Negra. I think I'd eat with a better appetite if I can find Mr. Foster and hand his glasses over to him.'

The taxi-driver did not know this suburb of Algiers well enough to take us direct to the Villa Negra. He had to ask his way several times, and at last stopped within sight of a white but rather neglected building which stood on a steep slope some way from the road.

The entrance gate which he had found was too narrow to admit a car, and the track beyond was little more than a path.

'*Ça alors,*' the driver muttered, and pushed his cap back on his head. 'After all that it is a back entrance!'

'That'll do,' I told him, and opened the door. 'We'll walk from here. How much do I owe you?'

The first part of the walk was easy. The ascent was only slight, though the path was overgrown with grass; brambles growing out from the bushes clawed at our clothes. Night had fallen long ago, but the windows on the ground floor of the Villa Negra were blazing and their reflected light illuminated the grounds.

As we came nearer we could see that the Villa had been a fine residence. It had a wonderful view out to sea and a magnificent terrace running along the whole front of the house. The ascent became steeper here, and the path weaved its way upwards in a series of little hairpin bends.

'It seems an odd way to call on strangers,' Steve whispered as we neared the top of the path. 'I can't help hoping that the genuine David Foster really is staying here.'

We both stopped short at the sudden burst of angry shouting which came from the front room of the house above us. At first the voices were muffled by the French windows which had been tightly closed. Then, as we stood staring upwards, we saw the shape of a man come hurtling through the glass, his arms held above his head in self-protection. A split second later the sound of a crash hit our ears, followed almost at once by the sharp bark of an automatic. The first shot was followed quickly by a second. From the man who had come through the window came a scream of agony.

We could see his shape outlined against the illuminated window. He was doubled up now, clutching at his stomach, running and stumbling towards the short flight of steps that led off the terrace on to the path which we were following. For a second he stood on the top step, fighting for breath, his body twisted with pain. Then he came plunging and slithering down. Without the light behind him we could no longer see him, but we could hear his sobbing gasps as he came nearer and nearer. Back at the house the French windows of the front room had been wrenched open and two men had stepped carefully out. But they seemed at a momentary loss in the darkness, and at first went casting off towards the wrong side of the terrace.

The fleeing man was on us before he saw us. So doubled up was he that he had no inkling of our presence till he saw our feet. Then he stopped and with great difficulty half straightened himself up. His head and hands had been viciously cut by the splintered glass. Blood was pouring down his face and from the tips of his fingers. But the real damage was being done by the lead bullet lodged in his stomach.

He swayed as he stood looking at us trying to make out whether we were friend or foe. I took hold of his arm to steady him. I thought his only chance of survival was to lie still and wait for medical help.

'Take it easy,' I said.

'Who are you?' the man said suspiciously. 'What are you doing here?'

There was something familiar about his way of speech.

I said: 'You're the man who telephoned me earlier this evening, aren't you? Is your name David Foster?'

He wiped a sleeve across his face to keep the blood out of his eyes. Had I not been holding on to him he would have fallen over. He was losing strength fast.

'You're Temple,' he gasped. I had to stoop as he sank down on one knee. 'I wish I could have got to you . . .'

His voice failed and he made a sudden grimace of pain. Steve was standing up staring towards the house.

'Watch out, Paul. They're heading back this way.'

I said urgently to the wounded man: 'Are you David Foster?'

'No. But it was me who telephoned you. He made me do it.'

He went down on the other knee and grabbed my arm as a shout sounded from the terrace above. Two forms in silhouette were at the top of the steps. One very tall, the other short and squat and somehow ape-like.

'Oh, God!' the man whispered hoarsely. 'Don't let them get me again.'

I looked down and saw with horror that a pool of blood was forming on the path where he knelt. He was losing blood terribly fast from some hidden wound.

'It's all right,' I tried to reassure him. 'We're going to take care of you.'

'Paul!' Steve hissed from close beside me. 'They're coming down the steps. What are you going to do?'

The wounded man heard her words. He made a supreme effort and half rose to his feet.

'Temple, whatever you do . . .' His voice was choking over the words. 'Whatever you do, don't let them have those spectacles.'

It was a final effort. He slumped, a dead weight on my hands.

I lowered him gently to the ground. Feet were already pounding on the path above, but we were screened by a bank of shrubs. I took the spectacles from my pocket and handed them to Steve.

'Steve. Take these and go back to the gate where we came in. Wait for me there. If I don't come within an hour go to the police and tell them everything.'

'Paul . . .' she began. 'I'm not going to leave you . . .'

'Go on,' I growled at her. 'Can't you see you're the only insurance policy I've got?'

I touched her arm, trying to speak less harshly. 'Please do as I ask.'

'God keep you,' she whispered as she took the glasses. A second later she had vanished into the bushes beside the pat. I knelt down quickly beside the wounded man. I thought that if I could do something to prevent him losing more blood he might still be saved. He was wearing no coat, just a thin shirt and a pair of trousers. Even his feet were bare. There was no sign of a shot wound on his front. Disregarding the approaching sound of feet and voices I rolled him over on his face. There was no resistance in him and he made no sound.

His back was matted with blood and the shirt was already stuck to his flesh in several places. I found it hard to account for the state of his shoulders unless he had been beaten or clubbed. I ripped the shirt apart and saw the hole where the blood was welling. I was making a pad with my handkerchief when the beam of a torch found and focused on me. The approaching footsteps stopped dead. For a moment the silence was heavy with menace. *'Qui êtes vous? Qu'est ce que vous foutez ici?'* The voice was harsh, the intonation and phraseology undeniably French.

'This man needs medical attention at once,' I said in English. 'Have you a telephone in the house?'

'I asked you who the hell you were,' the same voice said. This time he spoke in English, but with a trace of an American accent. 'What are you doing on my property? Is this guy a friend of yours or . . .'

The torch beam flicked down on to the wounded man. He was terribly still now. I put my finger on his pulse. There wasn't even a flutter.

'He isn't a friend of anyone now,' I said. 'He's dead.' I stood up wiping my hands clean on my handkerchief. The smaller of the two men came forward into the beam of the torchlight. He was a hunchback Arab with unnaturally long arms and huge hands. He turned the dead man on to his back without apparent effort and stared at his eyes.

'C'est vrai,' he muttered to the man holding the torch. 'Il est mort.'

I had somehow sensed, though I could not see it, that ever since the torch had found me I had been covered by the same automatic as had killed the man on the ground. I knew that I was a very unwelcome witness of the scene which had just taken place, and that the easiest solution for the man with the gun would be to shoot and dispose of me in the same way. I decided it was time I introduced myself. 'My name's Temple,' I began. 'I came here because this address was given me by a Mr. David Foster—'

'You are Temple?' The beam of light immediately moved from my hands up to my face. 'I am Colonel Rostand, the owner of this house. I am sorry that you have been given such an inhospitable welcome. This man broke into my house, but luckily we caught him red-handed. He managed to wriggle free and I took a pot shot at him more to frighten him than anything. I certainly never intended to hit him.'

'Two pot shots,' I corrected him. 'And I'm surprised to hear he wriggled free. To judge by his back he's been pretty thoroughly beaten up.'

'Well,' Rostand said. 'I'm afraid my man here is a little impulsive at times.'

The hunchback was watching me in a hungry kind of way, his great hands hanging limply by his thighs. He was turned half into the torchlight, and I could see that his forehead was unnaturally shallow and that his upper teeth protruded over his lower lip. I found myself thinking of Prospero and his creature Caliban.

The torch was abruptly switched away from me. Rostand had directed its light on to the path and turned back towards the house.

'I suppose I shall have to telephone the police and tell them that I've accidently shot a man. You'd better come up with me. I can introduce you to David Foster.'

'Then he is here?'

'Yes, of course,' Rostand said. 'He has been waiting for you to bring him his spectacles.'

As I moved to follow Rostand the Arab fell into place behind me. Like a sheep dog who senses his master's wishes he had guessed that I was not to be allowed to escape.

We passed into the house through the shattered French windows. The first room was a 'salon' furnished in a rather archaic style, like a room in a public museum. The chairs and tables were obviously genuine period pieces, but they were in a dilapidated condition. Rostand led the way through into a smaller room, the walls of which were lined with dusty books.

'If you will excuse me for a moment I will telephone the police. Sandro will attend to your needs.'

He gave the hunchback a significant nod, went back through the door and closed it.

Sandro's idea of attending to my needs was to stand, back to the door, with dangling arms and unblinking eyes fixed on my face. To avoid his scrutiny I turned to the shelves and picked out a book at random. It was Marivaux's *Les Fausses Confidences*.

I had time to read the first scene before Rostand returned. He was all affability now and had resumed the veneer of militarized good-breeding. He was tall and spare, very upright in his carriage, with a straggly brown moustache and perfectly round but very small steel-rimmed spectacles. His Adam's apple was noticeably pronounced; it jumped up and down when he talked. His hands were very restless, the fingers ceaselessly moving even when he was not using them.

'The police are coming,' he assured me with a smile. 'They say they recognize the man from my description. He's a notorious burglar whom they have been hunting for some time. I told Foster you were here. He'll be down in a minute.'

He turned to the Arab and spoke curtly in French.

'Ça va, Sandro. Tu peux partir maintenant.'

Without a word Sandro turned on his heels and went out through the door. He was about to close it when he stopped and pushed it back to allow another man to enter.

Rostand turned with an affable smile. 'Ah, Foster,' he said. 'This is your long-awaited friend, Mr. Temple.'

The newcomer stopped dead and stood frozen in the doorway, the hand he had already stretched out poised in mid-air. We stood contemplating each other for a few seconds.

'So this is David Foster?' I said to Rostand.

'Haven't I already told you so?' Rostand spoke impatiently, but he was puzzled by the attitude of both of us.

'You should have introduced yourself in Nice, Mr. Foster,' I said politely. 'But perhaps you did not feel the need of your glasses then. Your eyesight seemed to be functioning particularly well.'

The man who had introduced himself as Sam Leyland shrugged his shoulders heavily and glanced accusingly at Rostand.

'You should have warned me,' he said.

'Warned you of what?'

'That this was the same bloke as I met in Nice. We were both in the same hotel there.'

Rostand made one last attempt to take a grip on the situation.

'I don't know what he was calling himself in Nice, Mr. Temple, or why he did not introduce himself to you by his proper name. But I assure you that this is David Foster. Now if you will kindly hand over his spectacles I will have Sandro drive you home and you need not be involved in these tiresome formalities with the police.'

Sam Leyland was looking at me entreatingly, as if begging me silently to do as Rostand said and get out of the place. I shook my head.

'I'm sorry, Colonel Rostand, but I can't do as you suggest. For one thing I don't believe that this is David Foster. For another I don't believe that the man you shot is a common burglar. I prefer to believe that he is the person who telephoned me at the Aletti Hotel at twenty-past seven this evening, purporting to be David Foster. What happened? Did Sandro's impulsiveness make him unfit for public appearance?'

Though he hardly seemed to have made any movement the automatic suddenly appeared again in Rostand's hand. The pose of gentleman was abruptly abandoned.

'All right, Temple,' he said. 'You chose to have it this way yourself.'

He shaped his lips and gave vent to a shrill and piercing whistle such as a shepherd uses to control his dog. Instantly the door crashed open and Sandro erupted into the room. He saw that Rostand had me covered with the automatic, and moved without hesitation. With a muzzle pointing at my stomach and the memory of that pitiful figure lying on the path outside I was in no mood to resist. Even so I doubt if I could have done much in the grip of Sandro. His strength was enormous as he seized my arms, dragging them behind me and pinioning my wrists in the grip of one huge hand. The other arm went round my throat from behind, the hard bone of the forearm forcing my head back, almost closing my wind pipe. There was no denying that Sandro was impulsive.

'Come on, Leyland,' Rostand commanded. 'Frisk him.'

The slow-thinking Leyland moved forward. While Sandro held me arched backwards like something from the armoury of Robin Hood, he went carefully through my pockets. He turned unhappily to Rostand.

'He hasn't got them on him.'

'I could have saved—' I began, and at once Sandro's forearm tightened on my windpipe and the sentence ended in a gurgle.

'*Laisse-le parler,*' Rostand said. The grip relaxed again.

I said: 'I was only going to tell you that I could have saved Sam the trouble. I have not got the glasses with me.'

Rostand nodded.

'I suppose that was to be expected. The main thing is that we have you, and that is almost as good. Now I know Sandro will be disappointed if you tell me where to find them, because I have already denied him the pleasure of breaking one man's back this evening, but it will save the rest of us a lot of trouble—'

'You don't think I came up here without taking some elementary precautions,' I said. 'If I am not back at my hotel within half an hour the police will be informed exactly where I am.'

Again Rostand nodded as if conceding a putt to a golf opponent.

'You may be bluffing, but again you may not. I think I can afford to be generous. Perhaps after all we can come to a business agreement.'

'Then tell your Arab friend to unhook himself from my neck.'

'Tu peux filer, Sandro. Tu sais ce que tu as à faire.'

Sandro's arms slid away from my throat and my hands were released. So tight had his grip been that I had to rub my wrists to restore the circulation. I felt a good deal less unhappy when I heard the door close on him.

'Now then, Mr. Temple. I don't know what your interest is in this matter or why you should be so obstinate in refusing to hand over a pair of spectacles. But every man has his price. I will pay you five thousand pounds in British five-pound notes the moment I have possession of the spectacles. Of course you will still have the problem of getting the currency back to England. On the other hand if you are prepared to trust me I will have the money paid into any bank you mention.'

'I don't think much of your offer,' I said. 'Mr. Constantin was able to do much better. His figure was ten thousand.'

For the first time Rostand was rocked.

'Constantin?' His eyes switched to Leyland for an instant and then back to me. The fingers gripping the automatic had tightened. 'Did you sell the glasses to him?'

I knew that if I answered in the affirmative my number would be up. Rostand could have no further interest in keeping me alive and every reason for wanting me dead. On the other hand I was not prepared to give way to his threats or accept his offer. I calculated that not more than twenty minutes had passed since Steve and I had parted. If she followed my instructions the police could not be notified for another forty-five minutes. I doubted my ability to stall for as long as that, but it was worth trying.

'You said every man has his price. Mine is pretty high. I admit that I agreed to Constantin's figure, but if you are prepared to go higher than that – say twelve thousand five hundred.'

Rostand pounced quickly.

'Then you still have the spectacles.'

'Not exactly,' I hedged. 'They are at the moment in transit, but I think I can stop them before they reach him—'

'You're lying,' Rostand snapped suddenly. 'I'm not such a fool as you take me for. You haven't had any offer from Constantin, and the only offer you'll get from me is a bullet in your guts. Now start telling the truth quickly, or by heavens I'll give you the same treatment as Thompson. You saw how he finished up. You've just five seconds before I pull this trigger. One . . .'

There was no doubt in my mind that Rostand was ready to carry out his threat. There is an unmistakable look in a man's eyes when he feels the lust to kill.

'Two.'

Leyland had backed away and was watching apprehensively. He had probably seen the business with Thompson, and was sickening at the prospect of watching another man squirm to death.

'Three.'

I knew that the obvious thing was to tell a lie, but I funked it in the face of that supreme menace. There is a saying that a man on his death-bed speaks only the truth. I can confirm it from my experience at the Villa Negra. The temptation was very strong to tell them about Steve, standing not two hundred yards away with the glasses in her handbag. I had to bite my lips, knowing that the only thing was to keep silent, hoping that Rostand's nerve would break.

'Four.'

At the same instant as the word was spoken a telephone bell rang in the big front room we had come through. It might have been someone ringing the wrong number, but it was still enough to stop Rostand. I've often thought since how powerful the anonymity of the telephone bell is.

'See who it is,' Rostand snapped at Leyland.

The big man lumbered out of the room, glad to be spared the execution scene. The door swung behind him till it was almost closed. We could only hear the mumble of his voice as he answered. Rostand still kept me covered, but I was glad to note that he moved a little closer to me as he approached the door, straining to hear what Leyland was saying. That movement brought him within seven feet of me.

The conversation was brief. I heard Leyland walking hurriedly across the parquet floor. Rostand had to move away as he burst into the library. That brought him six inches nearer me.

59

'It was Constantin,' Leyland said excitedly. 'Temple must have been telling the truth. He says he has the glasses and is prepared to consider offers for them—'

This unexpected confirmation of what I had told him led Rostand to make his mistake. His gun hand wavered as he glanced in surprise towards Leyland. I knew it was my one chance, and that I must take it.

I brought my right foot up in a straight-legged rugger kick aimed at the automatic. It caught Rostand's hand and sent the gun sailing into the air. I was off balance for the moment, thrown forward with my head down. Rostand's fist was raised to strike as I straightened up. I brought the sharp point of my elbow up and drove it on to his chin with all the strength of my shoulder. I heard his jaw-bone crack and the crunch of his teeth as they came together. His head jerked back.

I had no more time for him at the moment. Leyland was coming for me, and I knew now how he had acquired that broken nose. He was a heavyweight boxer coming out of his corner to administer the knock-out to an opponent. They call boxing the Noble Art of Self Defence, but boxing is far too clean a sport to deserve that name. Boxers develop instincts which leave them wide open to an unfair attack. And believe me, when your life is at stake you are prepared to fight unfairly.

I went in below his guard and doubled him up with a blow for which the fans at Harringay Arena would have torn me limb from limb. As he went to the floor I stole a glance at Rostand. He was holding his jaw and stumbling towards the automatic, which lay at the base of one of the bookcases. I beat him to it and kicked the thing far out of reach. Rostand was clawing at me with his nails. He had bitten the tip off his tongue and blood was dribbling down his chin. I did not want to break my fingers on his jaw, so I chopped him on the neck with the side of my hand. His knees buckled and he slumped to the floor.

Leyland was still groaning and twisting his face with pain. I felt no compunction. My main worry was that Sandro would hear the din and come back. I had to hurry, and the memory of Thompson hardened my heart. The big Lancashire man stumbled to his feet and aimed a punch at me as I approached him. I let the blow go past my head, using his own strength to put a lock on his arm which almost pulled it out at the socket. He gave a yelp and began to dance on tip-toe.

'Now then,' I told him. 'You're going to do some talking. I advise you to answer my questions quickly.'

Just to encourage him I increased the pressure a little. He nearly rose off the ground.

'Why is Rostand so keen to lay hands on these spectacles? What is their value to him?'

'I don't know,' Leyland grunted. 'He never told me why he wanted them. He just said a friend of his had lost a very special pair of spectacles and was prepared to pay £4,000 to whoever recovered them.'

'And you were prepared to swallow that one? Surely you guessed that there was something fishy about that?'

'I did. But Rostand paid me a retainer of a thousand pounds, so why should I ask any questions? Here, go easy on my arm. I'm telling you the truth, aren't I?'

'I don't know,' I said, but I relaxed my grip a little.

'I didn't know it was going to be anything like this,' Leyland went on with a rush. 'Killing and all that. I had no part in what happened here to-night, I tell you straight.'

'Maybe not. But you're an accessory all the same. What were you doing at Nice?'

Leyland was silent and I had to put the pressure on again.

'All right, I'll tell you. Rostand tipped me the wink that a girl named Judy Wincott would be at the hotel in Nice on a certain night. He said she would be sure to have the spectacles. All I'd have to do was find out where her room was—'

'You knew Judy Wincott was going to be in Nice?'

'Yes. But I never saw her. I swear I didn't. She never registered at the hotel, you know. When I heard she'd been murdered I was . . .'

I found myself believing Leyland. He was a rogue but no murderer, and I could not help remembering the beseeching look he had given me when Rostand had offered me the chance of walking out of the house.

'You're really in trouble, Sam,' I said. 'Now what about David Foster? Have you ever met anyone of that name?'

Leyland shook his head.

'Rostand talked about him, but I never met him. I began to wonder if it was some code name.'

'Perhaps it is. All in all you don't know much, do you?'

'Too much for my liking,' Leyland complained with feeling. 'I wish I'd never set eyes on this Rostand.'

'How long have you known him?'

'No more than a month. I met him in Tunis through a business friend of mine.'

There were plenty more questions I wanted to ask Leyland, but Rostand was beginning to stir and I was always afraid that the formidable Sandro would reappear.

'One last question. Did Constantin say where he was speaking from?'

'No. He just asked Rostand to meet him at the El Passaro night club if he felt like talking business.'

'The El Passaro. Do you know it?'

'I don't know it, but I've heard of it.'

Rostand was grunting and spitting. I propelled an unre-
sisting Leyland into a large cupboard in the corner of the
room, pushed him inside and turned the key on him. The
automatic was still lying on the floor. I stared at it for only
a moment. Once again experience had proved my theory that
a gun only gives a man a sense of false security. I kicked it
out of sight under the heavy bookcase. Then I slipped out of
the library into the big salon. All the lights were still turned
full on. There was no sign of Sandro. I stepped out of the
French windows into the rapidly chilling night air.

When I reached the spot where I had parted from Steve
I stopped. I could just make out the dark, wet patch where
Thompson had lain, but his body had vanished. This must be
the work of Sandro, and since he had not returned to the house
he must have gone on towards the gate – where Steve was.

I ran rather than walked the remaining distance to the
gate, not caring about the branches and brambles which
clawed at my clothes and scratched my face. There was no
one in sight near the gate.

'Steve!' I called in a whisper. Then louder, 'Steve!'

A shadow moved out of the bushes and came towards me.

'Paul, thank God you've come! I was certain that something
had gone wrong with my watch. The time simply crawled.
What happened?'

'I'll tell you all about it later. You have the glasses safely?'

Steve nodded and touched her handbag.

'Better hand them back to me. Those spectacles are dyna-
mite to whoever has possession of them.'

She took them from her bag and I fitted them back into
their usual place in my handkerchief pocket.

'Did you see anyone go past while you were waiting?'

Steve shuddered at the memory.

'I did. A most awful hunchback Arab. He was carrying something over his shoulder. It looked like a body.'

'It was,' I said grimly. 'The body of our friend who came out through the French windows. Which way did he go?'

She pointed to a gate on the other side of the road. It was the twin of the one by which we were standing. By all appearances it was a private way down to the beach below.

'And he hasn't come back yet? Now I wonder what he's up to down there. It's going to be my word against three of them if they succeed in disposing of Thompson's body. Do you mind hanging on here just a little longer?'

'By myself? Yes, I do,' Steve said firmly. 'I was just about ready to scream when you came. If you're going down that path I'm coming with you.'

'All right,' I agreed after a moment. 'But keep well behind and don't make any noise.'

The gate uttered a mournful wail as I swung it open. I signalled Steve to leave it that way. Below on the beach we could hear the regular swish of small waves breaking on pebbles. Somewhere nearby there was stagnant water where frogs were croaking in raucous chorus. They all stopped to listen as Steve and I went stealthily by, and the sudden silence was unearthly.

Round a sharp twist in the steeply descending path we came in view of the beach. It was a small crescent-shaped miniature bay with a steeply shelving shore. At one side a pier had been built out to act at the same time as shelter for the boats and foundation for a small house. No boat was visible, the windows were dark, and there was no sign of anything moving.

But on the small expanse of pebbles by the pier, which seemed faintly luminous in the starlight, a lumpy object was lying. Cautioning Steve again, I slid down the rest of the path until my feet sank into the sand. I was near enough now to see that my first impression had been correct. The shape on the beach was that of a man.

Keeping a weather eye lifting towards the house, I moved cautiously towards him. He made no move, but I could hear the deep snoring breaths of a man who has been knocked out cold. The hunched back told me who he was, even before I was near enough to see the weal on the side of his forehead where he had been coshed. Even with his thick skull I thought he'd be out for a long time yet.

I left him where he was, and, signalling Steve to follow, approached the boat-house. Its windows were curtained and it had been freshly painted. It was in a far better state of repair than the Villa Negra. The windows were fastened and the door was locked. Using my pencil torch I inspected the lock. It looked like a simple job. Making use of a trick taught me by a professional burglar, I extracted a flat strip of celluloid from my wallet, and in a minute had the door open.

Very little light penetrated as far as the large sitting-room into which the door opened directly. I dared not switch on the lights even though there was a possibility that someone was standing there in the dark waiting for us. I ran the thin beam of my torch round the place, but it illuminated no crouching figure. A door at the far end was open and led into another smaller room.

It was early for anyone to be already in bed, but the moment I shone my light into the room I saw the shape of a form lying under the bedclothes. My instinct was to withdraw before he or she woke up and saw us. But something about the unnatural attitude of the form made me go closer. In the end I pulled the bedclothes back.

I thought then that I had found Thompson.

Yet this man was fully dressed and, what was more, he was wearing a jacket. I turned him over, and the beam of my torch drew a glint from the knife sticking into his ribs below the heart. It had been the professional killer's upward stab. I moved the torch beam up to illuminate his face.

'Constantin!'

I was so startled that I spoke the name aloud. To judge by the temperature of the body, allowing for the fact that he had been covered by the bedclothes, he had been dead for some time.

Who, then, had telephoned Rostand suggesting the meeting at the El Passaro? Who had killed Constantin and knocked out Sandro? And what had become of Thompson's body?

Steve, from the next room's windows, had been watching the beach. She came now to the door of the bedroom.

'Did you call, Paul? I think that Arab's beginning to come round. I saw him move just now.'

I had switched the torch off so that she would not see the body. I thought we had had our share of bodies for one evening, and that to delay longer would be tempting Providence.

'I have a feeling we may be over-staying our welcome,' I whispered to Steve. 'Let's get away from here while we still can.'

We had to walk some distance before we came to a main road, and I had ample time to tell Steve all that had happened from the moment we had separated.

'If Constantin's telephone call saved your life, then I'm sorry that he's dead,' she declared. 'However much of a crook he may have been.'

'But it can't have been he who telephoned,' I pointed out. 'He must have been dead already when that call was made.'

'Then presumably whoever killed him also telephoned Rostand. And that person will be at the El Passaro.'

'Which is exactly why you and I are going to pay the place a visit. Constantin's murderer can't know that I was at the Villa when he telephoned.'

'But wait a minute, Paul.' Steve slowed down a little. 'What's the point of arranging a meeting when he hasn't got the spectacles to sell? They are in your pocket.'

'He may have had a similar pair made, and be counting on hood-winking Rostand. As far as I can see, Steve, these spectacles have no special distinguishing feature.'

I grabbed her arm and hurried her into a run.

'Come on. There's a bus heading for the centre of the city. We can just catch it.'

Chapter Four

IT WAS eleven o'clock by the time we regained the Aletti Hotel and we still had not dined. My stomach was beginning to make empty rattling noises and Steve was having to stifle frequent yawns.

Even in the throes of this hectic crisis she was anxious to change into the appropriate clothes and put on her evening make-up before facing the public gaze at the El Passaro. I told her to go on up to our room while I went to have a talk with the receptionist. I was relieved to see it was the same man as had been on duty earlier that evening.

He answered my question before I asked it.

'Mr. Constantin found you, *monsieur*?' I stopped with one hand on the counter, startled at the way the answer to one of the night's mysteries had fallen into my lap.

'He was here, was he?'

'Yes, *monsieur*. He said it was very important that he should find you. I said that you had gone out to the Villa Negra.'

'That must have been pretty soon after we left.'

'Yes, *monsieur*. Hardly five minutes. I hope he found you all right.'

'Well, not exactly. It was rather a case of my finding him. But thanks, all the same.'

'You are welcome, *monsieur.*'

The clerk had already returned to his desk as I walked to the lift. The doors hissed across and the steel box moved imperceptibly upwards. So Constantin had followed us to the Villa Negra. And in that case someone else could equally well have followed Constantin – someone who stuck a knife under his ribs and hid him in the bedroom above the boat-house . . .

'*Quatrième, monsieur.*'

The tiny lift boy grinned as he announced my floor and stepped back to bow me out. Steve was already in her dressing-gown, and the sound of rushing water came from the bath-room. She took her evening dress in with her, closed the doors to keep out the sounds of bathing, and left me to place my call through to the police. The night duty inspector at the office of the *Police Judiciare* turned out to be one Flambeau, who, when I introduced myself, recognized my name.

It appeared that he had met Sir Graham Forbes, and even gone so far as to read a book of mine in order, he said opti-mistically, to improve his English. I gave him a brief summary of the situation and informed him that if his men were quick they would find one and perhaps two bodies at the Villa Negra.

'You might find it worthwhile to send a motor-boat with a searchlight round to the bay below Villa Negra. I have a feeling that you may find a boat drifting off-shore. I doubt whether you'll see much of Rostand or Leyland. But warn your men to watch out for a hunchback Arab. He's dangerous.'

'We will do our best,' Flambeau said with elaborate care. 'I know Rostand from your description. We have been watching him since 'e rented the Villa Negra. 'E is a known international criminal, but we did not know of what 'e was occupying 'imself thees time. You will come down to Police 'Eadquarters now, pleese?'

'I think it would be more profitable to meet at the El Passaro. Would it be possible for you to come there?'

'*Très bien*, since it is my Ministry which will pay. That is the most expensive place in Algiers.'

This time our instructions gave the French taxi-driver no cause for doubt.

'El Passaro?' he echoed, and clicked his meter on.

'You know it?'

'But naturally I know it. Up at Le Bardo.'

I handed Steve into the back and the taxi accelerated rapidly away. In a minute or two we were whistling up the road that climbs the hill at the back of Algiers. The lights of the harbour gradually fell away on our right. The rows of houses gave way to luxurious villas standing behind high railings in their own grounds.

I leaned forward to speak to the driver. There was no partition in the Ford Versailles.

'The El Passaro's a good place, I hear?'

'The hottest place in Algiers,' the driver said. 'This fellow Schultz has really made something of it. One thing you've got to give the Germans. When they do a thing they do it thoroughly.'

'Schultz. He's the proprietor, is he?'

'Yes. He was taken prisoner in the desert during the war, they tell me, and escaped – went and lived with the Arabs for several years. Now he has four of these places – here, Oran, Constantin, Tunis. Must make a packet out of it. This one's only been open six months, and as far as the smart set are concerned there is nowhere else in Algiers.'

'I hope you can eat there,' Steve interrupted with feeling.

The El Passaro Club was housed in what had till lately been the residence of a rich Arab merchant. The building was surrounded by magnificently kept gardens which Schultz had artistically flood-lit. The line of cars drawn up near the entrance gave testimony to the wealth of his clientele – Delahayes, Mercedes-Benz, an Alfa-Romeo and a number of the most recent American models. As soon as the taxi stopped outside the brilliantly illuminated entrance our door was opened by a boy with jet-black skin and gleaming white teeth. He wore a white silk turban and sky-blue, three-quarter length satin coat.

Once inside Steve was spirited away into what might have been a harem.

I caught a glimpse of veiled female attendants with billowing trousers and bare tummies. My own hat was taken by a magnificent brute in the traditional costume of a Touareg. Schultz had really gone to town on his Arabian Nights atmosphere.

Rich Kairouan carpets cushioned the steps that led down to the room where a tango orchestra was dreamily playing. Whereas outside the emphasis was on bright lights, the interior was almost as dark as a cinema. Veiled red electric bulbs, a few naked flames in ornate brass lamps, and here and there the orange flame of a waiter's chafing dish, showed the tightly packed tables and the mass of swaying couples on the dance-floor. The guests spoke in hushed voices. To say that the atmosphere was intimate is putting it mildly.

The *maître d'hôtel* standing at the top of the short flight of steps wore the bow-tie and tails which are traditional for his office. He greeted me with a smile, but shook his head regretfully when I asked him about a table for two.

71

'*Je regrette, monsieur.* All tables are already retained. There is nothing I can do for you.'

'Has *Monsieur* Constantin reserved a table? Perhaps he would not mind if we shared his.'

'*Monsieur* Constantin? You are a friend of his?' The *maître d'hôtel* was scrutinizing me more closely, trying to make out if he had seen me before. 'Wait one moment please.'

He darted away quickly, weaving a path between the tables like a snipe. He approached a man who was standing watching the dancers with a contented smile. They exchanged a few words, then both turned to move in my direction. I guessed by the deferential way in which the *maître d'hôtel* took second place that this was Schultz himself. My surmise was confirmed when he came near enough to speak.

He was a big, fair-haired man who carried himself like an athlete. His eyes were blue, his skin sun-burned and clear. I thought he was probably a good deal older than he looked. His clothes were immaculate and very well cut, and he wore them with considerable poise. He exuded confidence and force of character.

His smile came readily, yet he could not mask the faint suspicion of sneer which took the sincerity out of it. He had already made up his mind that I was English.

'You asked about a *Monsieur* Constantin, sir? I am afraid no one of that name has booked a table. I would like to help you, but as you can see we are very full up.'

His English was remarkably good, with just that faint stiffness which often characterizes the German who speaks our language.

'Perhaps there is a bar where we could have a drink? I arranged to meet a friend here.'

Instead of answering, Schultz half turned from me and executed a graceful bow. The *maître d'hôtel* did likewise. Steve had emerged from the ladies' room. I was forced to agree now that the time she had spent in changing her clothes had not been wasted. With her dangling ear-rings, the diamond brooch flashing on her bosom, and the swishing, tight-waisted taffeta dress, she looked both youthful and distinguished.

'*Madame,*' Schultz said in a slightly changed voice. 'I am sorry that I must keep you waiting for a moment, till we can find a table.'

Steve smiled forgivingly on him, and then glanced over my shoulder. Her eye had been caught by a man seated at one of the tables, who was waving at us.

'Isn't it Tony Wyse?' she said. 'I believe he's asking us to join him.'

Wyse it was, and a moment or two later the waiters had brought up two extra chairs and we were seated at his table. The fourth chair, I noticed, remained empty.

'What a fortuitous coincidence!' Wyse beamed on us happily. 'But, of course, everyone comes to the El Passaro. But everyone! I heard about it as far away as Paris. Waiter! *Encore une bouteille de champagne.*'

'It was kind of you to rescue us,' Steve said. 'I hope we're not intruding on your party.'

'Far from it,' Wyse said, and glanced at his watch. 'I was beginning to feel a trace of loneliness. My partner doesn't seem to be going to turn up.'

The tango orchestra finished its number with a long chord and the dancers began to move reluctantly off the floor. The drummer executed a roll, a spot-light blazed down, and Schultz stepped into the middle of the empty space.

'*Messieurs, Mesdames, Mesdemoiselles* – I present to you Yatisha – Queen of the Ouled Nails.'

There was a burst of mild masculine applause. The French business men at the back of the room clambered on to their chairs for a better view. An unseen four-man band began to play Arab music. On to the dance-floor whirled a dark-skinned girl. Her face was veiled and she wore gauze trousers, fastened at waist and ankles. For ten minutes she whirled and twisted, her hips and shoulders vibrating at unbelievable speed. It was an odd mixture of crudeness and art, strangely exciting. When at last she sank writhing to the floor, three middle-aged gentlemen at the back of the room fell off their chairs in their efforts to see better.

The applause was dying away when I saw that the waiter was pulling back the empty chair. A girl in a white dress with a wispy veil floating round her shoulders was picking her way gracefully between the tables. I saw Wyse scramble to his feet and I instinctively did the same. The girl raised her head and the reflection of the spot-light gleamed on her ash-blonde hair. She extended a hand to Wyse, who put his head over it and kissed it.

'Simone,' he said. 'I think you already know Mr. and Mrs. Temple.'

Simone Lalange was a little disconcerted to find that she was not going to have Wyse all to herself. There was an awkward little silence when we all sat down again. More to fill it than for any other reason, Steve said: 'I didn't know you two were so well acquainted.'

'It's a new friendship,' Wyse said in his curiously pedantic way, 'but a rapidly ripening one. Mademoiselle Lalange and I find we have a lot of interests in common.'

They smiled warmly at each other. I was about to ask Steve to dance, so that the other two could hold hands in peace, but at that moment a voice spoke in my ear.

'You are Mr. Temple, sir?'

It was Schultz. I said: 'Yes.'

'Monsieur Flambeau is here and would like a word with you.'

I excused myself and followed Schultz across the room and up a small flight of stairs. It led to a bar which looked down on to the restaurant, like a minstrel's gallery. There were several heavily curtained little cubicles where intimate conversations could be held. In one of these Flambeau was waiting for me.

Before Schultz left us I asked him if he would do me a favour.

'Always ready to be of service, sir.'

'Would you try and find out if there is anyone of the name of Constantin dining here?'

'I will do what I can, sir.'

He bowed himself out with mock servility, and I turned to shake hands with the man from the *Police Judiciare*.

'I regret you are waiting since a long time, Mr. Temple. I 'ave thought it best to go with the party to the Villa Negra.'

I liked Flambeau from the start. He was young and clearly highly intelligent. He might easily have been an army officer and not a police detective. Tall, quietly dressed and clean-shaven, he seemed to regard the world with a slightly amused tolerance.

I said: 'Did you have any luck?'

'So-so. It was a good idea to send the boat. They found a canoe drifting at a little distance from the beach. There was a – what do you call *cadavre?*'

'A body.'

75

'There was a body in it. It is to be supposed that it is the man called Thompson, but 'e 'as not been identified.'

'What about the other one? The fully-dressed man in the bed.'

'Yes. We found 'im. 'E is not known to us, but I 'ave sent the description to Interpol in Paris. Perhaps they can inform us something about 'im.'

'I can tell you one of his aliases. On the aircraft coming over he was calling himself Constantin.'

''E was on the aircraft with you?' Flambeau said quickly. 'Did you see 'im at Nice? Was 'e in the 'otel there?'

'Ah, *Inspecteur*. I see you have been checking up on my documents. Or has *Inspecteur* Mirabel sent you some advance information?'

Flambeau reddened a little, and I liked him better when I saw that he was genuinely embarrassed.

'We are constantly in communication,' he said quietly. 'Especially now that there is all this trouble with the *indigènes*.'

He drummed with his nails on the table top to reassert his authority, and switched the conversation back.

'I am afraid that we did not capture Rostand or his two accomplices. They 'ad vanished from the Villa. There were no traces of them.'

'That doesn't surprise me. I had the impression that they were merely camping in the Villa. I'm interested to hear that you already had your eye on Rostand.'

'We 'ave been watching 'im since 'e turned up 'ere a few weeks ago and rented the Villa. This is the first evidence we 'ave 'ad of 'is criminal activities. Now, please, you will be good enough to tell me why you went to the Villa Negra in the first place. What is this *histoire* of the spectacles?'

I gave Flambeau a rapid but comprehensive outline of the events as they had occurred so far. When I came to my visit to the Villa Negra he asked me for detailed descriptions of the persons I had met. He made careful notes and I tried to stick to the accepted police formula for descriptions.

'This will be a considerable 'elp,' he said, and I wished that I could tell him about his aitches. As he admitted to reading one of my books I felt somehow responsible for his English. It would have been quite good if he could have eradicated that one mistake. 'I do not think we will 'ave difficulty in arresting the malefactors—'

He broke off and touched my knee in warning. Schultz had mounted the stairs again and was coming towards us.

'I am sorry to disappoint you, sir. There is no one called Constantin in the restaurant as far as I can ascertain.'

'Well, thank you all the same.'

'Not at all, sir.'

Schultz was turning away when Flambeau called to him. 'One moment, please, *Monsieur* Schultz. I understand that you are acquainted with Colonel Rostand.'

I glanced at Flambeau and then turned to watch Schultz's face. Flambeau had not told me about this. The German was still smiling, but there was a wariness about his expression.

'He has invited me to the Villa Negra on one or two occasions. He is a very good customer of mine.'

'When did you last see him?'

Schultz thought for a moment.

'Perhaps a week ago.'

'You have not seen him this evening?'

'Of course not.'

'Or received any messages?'

77

'Excuse me, *Inspecteur*. May I know the reason for all these interrogations about Colonel Rostand?'

'He is wanted by the police,' Flambeau said shortly. 'And I warn you that if he comes here you must immediately inform the authorities.'

'But of course,' Schultz appeared to be deeply shocked and surprised at the news. 'What crime is the Colonel accused of?'

'Murder,' said Flambeau curtly.

Schultz regarded him with more humour than astonishment.

'Come, *Inspecteur*! You are pulling my leg. You cannot expect me to believe this of Colonel Rostand.'

'Believe it or not,' retorted Flambeau, 'but remember anyone who suppresses information about him will be considered an accomplice.'

He nodded to show that the interview was over. Still with that slightly sneering smile on his face, Schultz withdrew.

'I am curious to see these spectacles,' the *Inspecteur* went on when we were alone again. 'You have them with you?'

Once again the spectacles were produced and handed from hand to hand. Even I, whose mind carried a permanent picture of them, found myself scrutinizing them afresh.

'There is nothing remarkable about these,' Flambeau said as he handed them back to me. 'I cannot believe that they are in any way connected with these crimes.'

'Perhaps not. None the less I shall be very glad when they're off my hands. We're flying on to Tunis to-morrow and I can tell you that the first thing I'll do when I get there is to find the real Mr. David Foster.'

When I returned to the table I found Simone Lalange sitting alone. Tony Wyse, gallant gentleman that he was, had decided that Steve was due for a turn on the floor. I could see them close to the orchestra, laughing at some joke he had made and getting along very well together.

The least I could do was ask the French girl to dance. She gave me the full force of her dazzling smile and accepted with enthusiasm.

I think I would have enjoyed the dance more if I had not suspected that Steve's eyes were occasionally on me. For Simone Lalange dancing was no conventional contact of hand with hand. She snuggled close against me, and when her hair tickled my chin I breathed in some subtle perfume reminiscent of pine-smoke and lotus ponds. There was no question of making polite conversation. This was an intimate, secret experience implying an understanding deeper than words.

At one moment she suddenly moved away from me and seemed to be looking at my breast pocket.

When the music ended she disengaged herself with slow reluctance and we threaded our way back to our own table. Just before we reached it two waiters, each moving fast in the opposite direction, collided violently. One of them raised his fist, struck the other, and sent him crashing to the ground. A woman screamed and Simone clung to me. Immediately all the electric bulbs in the room went out so that the darkness was almost total. I felt a surge of bodies jostling around me, then something heavy thumped me on the chest and I was borne to the ground. Instinctively my hand went to my handkerchief pocket.

The spectacles had already gone!

Feverishly I groped round the floor on my hands and knees, but only had my fingers stamped on for my pains. Several women were screaming now and there was a crashing sound as tables were overturned. Above it all a man was shouting at everyone to keep calm.

Then abruptly the lights came on again, this time reinforced by a huge chandelier in the centre of the ceiling.

Schultz had leapt on to the band's platform.

'Everything is all right,' he shouted. 'It was just a blown fuse!'

He made a signal to the band leader, who raised his baton to start the next tune. People began shamefacedly to resume their seats, waiters to pick up the fallen crockery. There was no point in my searching the floor for the spectacles. They could not have fallen accidentally from my pocket. The rest of our party were collecting round the table, laughing and joking over the incident. Steve saw by my look that something had gone wrong. She moved quickly to my side.

'What's happened, Paul?'

'The spectacles. They've gone. Someone must have taken them from my pocket when the lights went out.'

'You're sure they're not there?'

'Of course I am.' I patted the empty pocket where the spectacles had been. 'I wonder if Flambeau's still here. Perhaps we could have the exits sealed.'

'What's the trouble?' Wyse said. 'Lost something?'

'Yes,' Steve said. 'My husband lost a pair of spectacles.'

On the other side of the table the French girl was just putting away her mirror after re-arranging her hair and touching up her lips.

'We'll ask the band leader to make an announcement,' Wyse said. 'Someone's sure to find them. Nothing else missing? Putting the lights out may have been a pickpocket's trick.'

'My handbag!' Steve said. 'I'm sure I left it on the table in front of my place.'

Wyse pulled her chair back and stooped to look under the table.

'Here it is,' he said, and picked the small black evening bag off the seat of the chair. 'Better check and see if anything's missing.'

Steve took the bag, opened it, looked inside and then slowly raised her eyes. Her expression was very puzzled. She lifted out the spectacles and handed them to me.

'Just like a wife!' Wyse laughed. 'She must have had them all the time.'

'Well, Paul. Here we are at last. I wonder if the real David Foster is waiting for us down there.'

I glanced at Steve as she sat opposite me looking cool and poised in an exquisite white suit and wondered, not for the first time, at her ability to bob up so freshly after a night of adventures.

Our aircraft was banking over the luxury suburb of Sidi bou Saïd before making its run in to El Aouina airport. Ahead of us, with a faint haze dancing over the roof tops, the modern city of Tunis lay spread out below the ancient Kasbah. The waters of the bay were a greeny blue, flecked here and there by a white-crested wave. Within the inner bay the water was flat and calm, its surface bisected by the railway running out to Khérédine. We flew in low over the arena of Carthage and caught a glimpse of the aqueduct along which the Romans had brought their drinking water from the mountains of Zaghouan.

Many of the passengers on this flight had been our companions on the Nice to Algiers hop. A notable absentee was Constantin. Wyse and Simone Lalange were seated further forward in the plane. The young man had been successful in having his seat moved so that he could be beside her.

I had been watching Mademoiselle Lalange with a good deal more interest since the incident in the El Passaro. It would have been easier for her than for anyone else to have removed my precious spectacles when the lights went out. But if she had done so what was the point of planting them in Steve's handbag? The idea of a substitution had occurred to both of us. I had, however, taken the precaution of placing a very clear thumb print on the inner face of one of the lenses. On returning to the hotel I had applied white dust to it and confirmed that it was still there. My thumb print was one identification mark which no one could detect at a casual inspection and which was impossible to fake.

Our pilot made heavy weather of his landing. We hit the runway with a tremendous bump, and for a sickening moment went flying through the air again before he got us down. Most of the passengers were looking a little green when the machine came to a standstill and the hostess opened the door.

The Tunisian authorities were maddeningly officious, and it took us a long time to pass through the customs and immigration checks. Wyse, with his plausible way of talking and his condescending manner, rubbed them up the wrong way completely. They examined every article in his baggage with minute care and even insisted on him emptying his pockets. When at last we were clear I made a point of looking at the notice-board where messages for arriving travellers are posted. There was nothing for us. Nor did anyone appear to have come out from the city to meet this particular plane.

I noticed Wyse saying a regretful farewell to Simone Lalange. She had insisted on taking a taxi on her own, and Master Wyse was not being allowed to accompany her. He watched her enter the back seat with a flash of high heels and silken legs, and soon after she had driven away he called up a taxi for himself.

Steve and I waited about for a little time to give David Foster every chance of making contact with us if he was there. By so doing we missed the free bus-ride into Tunis and we too had to charter a taxi.

Tunis was somehow more open and clean than Algiers, and there was not the same tense atmosphere here. There were a great many people in Western clothes about, but the Arabs had a more prosperous air and held their heads higher.

We had booked a small suite at the Hôtel François Premier, which stands in the Avenue Jules Ferry. As our baggage was being taken up I asked for a telephone directory, and turned to the names beginning with 'T'.

'Well, here's Trans-Africa Petroleum anyway,' I said to Steve, with my index finger under the entry. '*120* Avenue de Rome. Make a note of the number for me, will you?'

Siesta time in Tunis continues until about four, so I had to possess my soul in patience until the hour struck. It would have been a waste of time to telephone any office until then.

At five minutes past I put the call through. I was answered by the mechanical voice of a switch-board operator.

'I would like to speak to Mr. Foster, please. Mr. David Foster.'

My request met with no acknowledgment, but I heard a series of clicks and then a prolonged buzzing. At last a man's voice spoke sleepily.

'Forster here!'

'My name's Temple,' I said. 'I expect you've had a message from Judy Wincott about me. I'd like to make an appoint—'

'Judy who?'

The voice at the other end sounded very angry, as if its owner had only just woken up and didn't like what he saw.

'Judy Wincott. I happened to meet her in Paris and she asked me to return your spectacles to you.'

'Look here!' the voice spluttered. 'Is this some kind of joke? I've never heard of any Judy Wincott, and the only pair of spectacles I've got are firmly planted on my nose.'

'But you are David Foster?'

'My name is Daniel Forster – with an *r*. Now if you'll kindly get off the line—'

'Just a moment,' I said quickly, before he could hang up. 'This is really rather important. Is there anyone called David Foster in your Company?'

'No,' Mr. Forster said emphatically. 'If there was I'd know him. I'm the Personnel Manager.'

Chapter Five

'WELL,' I said as I replaced the receiver. 'That's that.'

'No David Foster?'

'No David Foster. The nearest I could get was a Mr. Daniel Forster.'

'But that's almost the same name, Paul. Mightn't Judy Wincott have made a mistake?'

'Judy Wincott might, but not Daniel Forster. His spectacles are firmly planted on his nose and something in his voice implied that it would take a platoon of paratroopers to get them off. No, Steve, I'm certain he's nothing to do with this business.'

'Perhaps he's being used in some way without knowing it.'

'No. I think it's just a coincidence. Not really that, even. I dare say there's someone with a name vaguely like David Foster in every organization as big as Trans-Africa Petroleum.'

Steve moved to the window and began to wind up the slatted shade that had protected the room from the fierce midday heat. The reflected light from the white houses opposite flooded in.

'In that case, who and where is the real David Foster?'

'I don't believe he exists.'

'You mean the whole story was invented?'

'Maybe. On the other hand maybe David Foster is dead. What I do believe is that a very carefully conceived plan has gone wrong somewhere – and you and I are left holding the baby.'

'The baby being the spectacles? So what are you going to do now? You can't very well deliver them to an owner who doesn't exist.'

I opened the wardrobe and took out a pair of mesh shoes with composition soles which I'd bought in Algiers. They would be a lot cooler than the brogues I had worn on the journey. I sat down on the edge of the bed and began to undo my laces.

'I suppose the correct thing would be to hand them over to the police as lost property. But I confess that would go against the grain. Have you noticed how many odd people have come into our lives since we've had those glasses? Sam Leyland, Tony Wyse, Constantin, Colonel Rostand – not to mention the inimitable Sandro.'

'And Simone Lalange,' Steve reminded me with a dark look. 'You needn't try and make me think you've forgotten about her.'

'No, I hadn't. You just didn't give me time to get to her.'

'Nor will I if I can help it,' Steve warned me. We both laughed.

I stood up and wriggled my toes. My feet were very grateful for the new shoes. They could bulge and breathe in them much more comfortably.

'I feel as if we're being accompanied by an invisible travelling circus, all pretending to be busily engaged in something else, but in fact with only one thought in their minds – these spectacles. No, I'm going to hold on to them. I shall be interested to see who is the next candidate for our friendship.'

I stood in front of the cheval mirror, wondering if the new shoes were too yellow. Steve came up behind me and put her hands on the sides of my arms. I could see her looking over my shoulder at our reflexion.

'I think you must be very careful, Paul. These people are prepared to kill each other. If you go too far they might decide to kill you too. I wish you wouldn't insist on carrying the spectacles round with you, darling.'

I turned round to face her.

'I don't think anything will happen for a while, Steve. A clumsy attempt was made in Algiers to persuade me to part with them. I believe that another and more subtle approach will be made here in Tunis. It's bound to involve a little preparatory work on someone's part. And I promise you that to-morrow, as soon as the banks open, I'll deposit these in the Lloyds branch here.'

I patted my handkerchief pocket gently. The spectacles hardly showed. I had cut a piece of cardboard to the right size and slipped it down outside the glasses. It acted at the same time as concealment and protection.

'Now,' I said. 'When you're ready . . .'

'When I'm ready?' Steve echoed. 'I've been waiting for five minutes. Who's been standing admiring his feet in the mirror?'

I opened the door and gave Steve a little push out into the corridor, then locked it behind us.

'Where to now?' she enquired.

'We came here to see Tunis, and that's what I suggest we do. Let's start by taking a stroll round some of the main streets. It's not too hot for walking now.'

The streets, which had been fairly free during the siesta hours, were now filling up rapidly. We crossed to the middle of the roadway and walked up the broad central pavement under the shelter of a double line of trees. The usual assortment of street hawkers tried to sell us guides, postcards, trinkets, Parker pens and Rolex Oysters. We stopped at a news stall to buy an evening paper, watched with interest while three sharp-eyed Arab boys shinned up an electric light standard to retrieve a model aircraft from a tree, risked our lives to get across the roadway again, and then started window-shopping along the Avenue de Rome.

We had just moved on from a window displaying beautifully made leather bags and suitcases of all shapes and sizes when I put my hand under Steve's elbow.

'We're being followed.' I felt her stiffen involuntarily. She knew better than to glance round.

'Already?'

'He may be an ordinary pick-pocket. There are always thieves hanging round the big hotels who trail tourists in the hope of catching them unawares. We'll give him an opportunity of coming to closer quarters.'

'What does he look like?'

'European. About five-foot-five, fiftyish, clean-shaven, grey ready-made suit about two sizes too big for him and a green felt hat.'

We took a turning to the right which would bring us back to the hotel, and continued to move along the street in the same halting way, pausing every now and then to gaze at a window display. Our shadow was far from expert, and I could see him reflected in a pane of glass with affected casualness whenever we stopped. I remembered that the Hôtel François Premier had a good American Bar with a separate entrance from the street. Steve and I paused outside it as if debating whether to go in, and out of the corner of my eye I could see our shadow watching us. When we entered I had no doubt that he knew where to find us if he wanted to.

The bar was still rather empty, but a radiogram was thumping gently and an Arab barman, in spotless white nylon jacket, was shaking a cocktail for two Sultans disguised as European business men. Steve and I took stools at the bar and ordered our usual Dry Martinis.

The barman was still shaking them up when in the mirror behind the bar I saw the little man in the big grey suit come in.

He made no bones about it. He marched straight up to the bar, hoisted himself on to the stool beside me, and nodded to the barman.

''Soir, Achmed. Oon Scotch avec Seltz, silver play.'

He spoke his piece with an atrocious French accent, then turned and winked broadly at me.

'Lovely weather we're havin'!'

The voice was thick and carried an aroma which told me that this was not his first Scotch of the evening. His accent was already unmistakable as a boggy Irish.

'Very good for the time of year,' I agreed politely, knowing perfectly well that during spring in Tunis the sun can be relied upon to shine all day from a clear sky.

'Is it here on holiday yes are?'

'That's right. Trying to find somewhere that isn't crowded with tourists.'

He nodded several times, acknowledging the wisdom of my observation. His blue and white striped shirt was not too clean, and the red and white tie seemed to be trying to draw attention away from it. He kept his hat on, tilted well to one side with the brim pulled rakishly down over a bloodshot eye. He hadn't shaved that morning, and I didn't think he'd dared to display his teeth to a dentist for ten years or more. They were brown with nicotine stain and one was missing from each row. The suit was a puzzle. I couldn't imagine anyone choosing a suit two sizes too big. In a way he looked as if the heat of Tunis had made him shrivel up and shrink inside it.

'Oh, ye've come to the right spot, then. It's a wonderful place, Tunis. But ye'll need to mind yer step, don't ye know. It doesn't do to be wanderin' about the native quarter after dark. There's many a one has gone lookin' for a bit of the Arabian Nights, don't ye know, and been found next mornin' . . .'

He broke off to bare his teeth with a rasping noise and draw a finger across his throat.

'You live here, I take it?' I asked him.

'O'Halloran's the name,' he said at once, and offered me a hand iodized with tobacco stain. 'Will this be your wife, now?'

'She is,' I affirmed, straightening him up on his tenses.

He slithered down off his stool and went to pump Steve's hand, while she looked down on him from the queenly loftiness of her perch.

'Isn't it the beautiful creature she is?' cried O'Halloran with enthusiasm. Steve was trying to pull her hand away, but the small Irishman would not part with it. I watched with interest to see if he would try and relieve her of her wrist-watch or dip into her handbag. 'Now don't tell me there isn't a bit of Irish in her with them eyes. There isn't? Ah, I'll not believe it. Thank you, Achmed. Merci. No! Go easy with the soda. Excuse me if I make a long arm. Ha! Ha! Well, here's to yer very good health and a pleasant stay in the city of Tunis. That's better. Will ye have an American cigarette?'

He smacked his lips and produced a battered packet of Camels from his pocket. Steve and I declined the offer. O'Halloran moistened his lips, inserted a cigarette between them, rotated it till it was thoroughly wet, then ignited it with a match, which he struck on the seat of his trousers by raising his right knee. He blew it out without removing the cigarette from his mouth, inhaled for about thirty seconds, and then began to talk. The smoke did not reappear until a good deal later in the conversation.

'Isn't it funny the way chance works out? Here yes are, sittin' havin' a drink, wonderin' how on earth yes are to find yer way round this strange city, and who should come along but meself – just the very man in the whole of Tunis who can do the most to help yes. Isn't it amazin' now?'

'You mean,' Steve said in a voice that trembled slightly with suppressed laughter, 'that you're a guide, Mr. O'Halloran?'

'*A* guide, me dear? Say rather, *the* guide. Sure I know Tunis like the back of me hand.' O'Halloran looked at the back of his hand, then put it quickly in his pocket. 'Or better, perhaps. Here, take a look at this.'

He whipped from his pocket a tattered wallet, bulging with letters, newspaper cuttings, business cards and even a few notes of currency. Carefully he took out a photograph cut from some newspaper years and years ago. It was yellow with age and coming apart at the line where it was folded. I knew that Mr. O'Halloran's eyes were upon me as I studied it. It showed a group of prosperous Americans lined up beside a charter aircraft. In the centre of them, like a monkey mascot, was Mr. O'Halloran in his prime of life.

'The United States Federation of Brewers and Bottlers. Picked me to be their official guide during the whole three days of their visit to Tunis.'

'That's a wonderful testimonial, Mr. O'Halloran. Look, darling, this is Mr. O'Halloran with the United States Federation of Brewers and Bottlers.'

'It's a very good likeness,' Steve said fatuously as she leaned across to study the picture.

'I'm glad you like it. And now . . .'

With equal care Mr. O'Halloran selected one of the business cards he carried in his wallet. He handed it carefully to Steve, who in her turn showed it to me.

HOUSE OF SHONI
(ZOLTAN GUPTE: ART DEALER)
227, Avenue Mirabar,
TUNIS
Curios a Speciality
American & English visitors
welcome.
Tel: 187592

Written across the top in a shaky hand were the words: 'Patrick O'Halloran. Special Representative.'

'It's well worth a visit,' the Irishman assured us with sudden earnestness. 'Indeed it'll pay you handsomely. I can show you the way to the place meself. When will it suit you to pay a visit?'

'Well, Mr. O'Halloran, our plans aren't quite definite yet. We'd prefer to look around on our own for a bit first. Then later we'd be very glad of your services. How can we get in touch with you?'

'Just ring that number. And remember – day or night, Pat O'Halloran is at your service. Yes won't forget now? The House of Shoni. I wouldn't delay it too long if I were you. And now, sir and madam, if yes will excuse me I have a party waitin' to be shown round the Kasbah.'

Mr. O'Halloran swept his hat off, revealing a mass of surprisingly youthful curls, gave us both a broad wink, and made his exit. He had not attempted to pay for his drink.

Steve and I both burst out laughing the moment he had gone.

'If I hadn't seen him with my own eyes I wouldn't have believed such a character existed,' she said. 'He was pure music hall.'

She slipped Mr. O'Halloran's card into her handbag.

'I mustn't lose this. Did you notice how vehement he was about our visiting the shop, Paul? Do you think there's anything significant about that?'

'Could be. We'll leave Mr. O'Halloran in the oven for a bit and let him cook. I somehow think he'll show up again before long.'

The bar was beginning to fill up now. It seemed to be one of the fashionable meeting places for the French inhabitants of Tunis. Most of them had sat at the small tables, and Steve and I were rather conspicuous at the bar. Mr. O'Halloran was not quite what I had expected, and I had a suspicion that there was someone in the bar who was waiting for the chance to speak to me.

'Steve,' I suggested, 'how would you like to go on up and start changing? I'll stay down here for a while. Someone we know may turn up.'

She gave me a quick look, but took the hint and climbed down from her stool.

'Can I have the key, please?'

I took the key from my pocket and handed it to her.

'See you in about twenty minutes. Another Dry Martini, please, Achmed.'

I was quite right in my suspicion that the young man sitting alone at one of the tables had been waiting for a chance to talk to me. Almost as soon as Steve had gone he came up and introduced himself. He had been in London on business at a time when I was engaged with Sir Graham Forbes of Scotland Yard on a murder case which had hit the headlines. He had seen my photograph at that time and remembered it. He was a likeable young Frenchman, and we were soon deep in a discussion about the possibilities created for international criminals by modern methods of travel and communication.

We had been talking for seven or eight minutes when I saw a woman come hurriedly into the American Bar through the curtained door which led to the hotel *foyer*. She was handsome rather than pretty, and fairly tall. At a quick guess I put her age down as thirty. She had a good figure but was built on generous lines. Her bones were large. Her clothes were severe though well-made. Black, close-fitting skirt, high-heeled shoes, white, crinkly shirt, expensive ear-rings. She was the type of comely but efficient secretary who wouldn't let her boss turn office hours into workers' playtime.

She glanced all round the room until her eyes came to rest on my faintly tweedy person. I suppose it was the cut of my jacket which gave me away. She came towards me, a worried frown on her carefully made-up face.

'Oh, *pardon, monsieur. Vous n'êtes pas, par hasard, Monsieur Temple?*'

Though she put the question in French the American accent was already apparent.

'Yes. My name is Temple.'

'Thank goodness I've found you, Mr. Temple, and excuse me butting in like this.'

She glanced at my companion, who had leapt to his feet and was standing to attention in expectation of an introduction.

'Is anything wrong?' I asked her, sensing the urgency in her manner.

'It's your wife. I'm afraid she's had a nasty shock. But she's quite all right. You can rest assured of that. I've given her a little sedative and she's lying down quite calmly now. I wouldn't have left her but she was most insistent that I should come and fetch you—'

'Excuse me, please,' I flung over my shoulder at the youthful criminologist, and began to hurry the secretarial young woman towards the door. He bowed stiffly and disapprovingly, and I knew that he thought the manners of the English were the absolute bottom.

'Are you on the staff of the hotel?' I asked the girl as we stood waiting for the lift to come down, which it did with agonizing slowness.

'No. I occupy the room next door to yours, Mr. Temple. I was lying down resting when I heard your wife scream—'

'Scream?'

The lift had arrived at last. The girl hurried in, I followed, and pushed my finger on the button for the third floor. When the doors had rolled across the lift began to move upwards.

'Of course I ran in straight away. Your wife was lying on her back on the bed, struggling with a man who was holding a pillow over her face—'

'By Timothy! Go on.'

'Well, that's about all. When he saw me he made a dash for the window and disappeared on to the balcony. I didn't try to follow him. I was too concerned about your wife. She was having difficulty in regaining her breath—'

'And you mean to say you left her alone in that room?' I began angrily.

The American girl looked at me reprovingly.

'I made sure the window was bolted, Mr. Temple, and I locked the door behind me. You can see I have the key here.'

95

'Sorry. It's just that I was rather horrified when you described—'

'There's no need to apologize.' A hand was laid gently on my forearm and I felt a slight pressure of fingers through my coat. 'You had a horrible shock. By the way, my name is Audry Bryce – *Miss* Audry Bryce.'

The lift doors slid back and I let her walk out ahead of me and lead me to the door of our room. She unlocked it, and this time stood back to let me enter first.

Steve was lying on the bed, but she sat up when she saw me. She was very flushed, and I saw at once that she was still trembling. *Miss* Bryce stood tactfully in the background while I made sure that I still had a wife in one piece. Then she coughed to remind us that she did exist.

'Well, I think I'll be running along now. I've put the key in the lock on this side.'

'Oh, please don't go yet,' Steve said. 'Paul, Miss Bryce has been terribly kind. I don't know what would have happened if she hadn't come to the rescue. I'm afraid I almost had hysterics on her.'

'Yes, we really are very grateful to you,' I said. 'You couldn't possibly dine with us this evening? We'd both enjoy it very much if you would.'

'That's very kind of you, Mr. Temple, but I'm afraid I have a previous engagement. Perhaps we'll have the pleasure of meeting later, though.'

'I hope so. And thank you again.'

As soon as the door had closed Steve swung her legs to the ground.

'Paul, do you know who the man was?'

'Now, Steve, how on earth could I—?'

'It was Sam Leyland.'

'Sam Leyland? Tell me exactly what happened.'

I sat down on the bed and eased Steve's head down on to the pillow.

'Well, I came up here, unlocked the door, walked in and closed it again – you know the way one does, without thinking. Then this figure sort of loomed up at me from behind the bed. He put his hand over my mouth. I bit it good and hard and he let go. That's when I got my screams in, and saw that it was Sam Leyland. Then he wrestled with me and threw me down on the bed. Oh, Paul, when he put the pillow over my face I began to think of Judy Wincott and the way we found her in that cupboard—'

'I wish I'd hit Sam harder at the Villa Negra. Did you get any idea of what he was doing here? The place does not look as if it has been searched.'

'I think I must have surprised him before he got started properly. Unless he really intended to suffocate me . . .'

I walked across to the French windows and unbolted them. The balcony, of course, was deserted; but it ran the whole length of the hotel and only a low wall separated the section belonging to each room.

'I don't believe he intended to harm you,' I said as I came back into the room. 'The pillow was to prevent you calling for help.'

'Then you think he was after the spectacles again. Surely they don't imagine we're going to leave them lying about in a hotel bedroom after all that's happened?'

'Perhaps they think we're less intelligent than we really are. How are you feeling now? Would you like a brandy or anything?'

Steve shook her head.

'I'm quite all right now. I really think I gave as good as I got. I wonder if I bit right through his flesh?'

97

'Blood-thirsty female! How would you like me to order dinner to be sent up here?'

'No, I wouldn't like that. I feel I want to get right away from this room. What I long for more than anything is pints and pints of good fresh air.'

'That's a rare commodity in Tunis, but I think I know the next best thing.'

When Steve was ready I took her down and we walked a little way up the street to a cab rank where a line of horse-drawn open carriages stood waiting. An Arab coachman, who looked every day of a hundred, clambered down from his seat to hand Steve up into the beautifully upholstered passenger compartment.

'You visit Kasbah, *monsieur*? Old part of Tunis?'

'Anywhere you like,' I said. 'Just as long as you keep moving.'

The whip cracked above the horse's head and we moved forward. The streets were in shadow now and the old horse drew us along fast enough to bring an aromatic but none the less agreeable breeze fanning round our cheeks.

For the next hour, lulled by the rhythmic clip-clop of hooves, we tried to forget all about murder and violence, and to conduct ourselves like a pair of unashamed tourists. Our coachman took us on what must have been his routine tour, and I was glad that no one in the streets we passed along took undue notice of his two fares. The sky had turned a deeper blue, and already in the east one bright star was twinkling. We passed along gay boulevards where the café tables on the pavements were crowded. Every now and again our driver would point to some fragment of a wall or to an archway which reminded the modern traveller that here, too, the Romans had been before him. At one stage we plunged into the narrow alleys of the old

Arab quarter, and a flock of yelling Arab boys began to run along behind the cab. Our coachman drove them off with his whip. The closely packed houses rose up sheer and dark on either side, so close that it would have been easy for anyone to throw solids or liquids out of the window on top of us. There were few Europeans in these streets. Ragged Arabs wrapped in their one-piece garments squatted at the foot of the houses on either side of the black doorways. Veiled women with only their eyes showing pressed themselves against the walls to leave us room to pass. We caught glimpses of squalid cafés packed with gossiping Arabs, and heard the curious wailing sound that passes for song in the Near East. Once we encountered a street fight of frightening violence. Razors and knives were out and we saw one man's forehead slashed to the bone. Our driver whipped his horse up and took us out of the trouble at a canter. All the time we were in the native part I had the sensation that hundreds of eyes were fixed on us; some with indifference, some with hostility, and some with a disturbing look of calculation. By the way she pressed closer against me I knew that Steve felt it too.

It was a relief when we suddenly emerged into a broader street and found ourselves back in the modern part of the city.

I paid the driver off at the point where we had started. Remembering the razors I gave him a good tip, and he heaped the blessings of Allah on both our heads.

'How's your appetite?' I enquired as we turned towards the hotel.

'I think I'm really hungry, though my tummy did some funny things when we saw that fight.'

'Then I suggest we go straight to the dining-room. Unless you want to go upstairs first?'

'No. I'm quite ready, as long as you don't mind eating with a shiny nose.'

I asked a *chasseur* the way to the dining-room, but we had not gone far towards it when a tubby man in a black coat and striped trousers came running after us.

'Mr. Temple!' His voice was urgent, but pitched very low as if he were passing me some secret message. '*Le Commissaire* Renouk has been waiting to see you. I did not know where to find you, and he is become terribly impatient. If you do not mind, *monsieur*, he is waiting in my office.'

We had already stopped dead in our tracks.

'*Le Commissaire* Renouk?' I echoed. 'Is he from the police?'

'*Oui, monsieur*. From the *Commissariat de Police*.'

'And does he want to see me or my wife as well?'

'Just you, *Monsieur* Temple, I think.'

'You are the Manager?'

'The Night Manager, *monsieur*.'

'You speak excellent English.'

The small man put his head on one side trying to look pleased and modest at the same time.

'*Monsieur* is too amiable.'

'Now, I'm going to place *madame* in your personal care while I am talking to the *Commissaire*. Will you make yourself responsible for her well-being?'

The Night Manager placed one hand on his diaphragm and the other hand on his kidneys before bowing low.

'*Enchanté, madame*. And now, *monsieur*, if you will please to come this way. *Monsieur le Commissaire* is already very impatient.'

The man I found waiting for me in the Manager's office had somehow succeeded in filling the small room with an atmosphere of disapproval, suspicion and menace. He was wearing a khaki uniform liberally adorned with gilt. Several meaningless medal ribbons meandered across his chest. He wore a French-style képi which he had kept on his head. His skin was sallow, his eyebrows very black and bushy, his mouth thin and twisted down on one side.

'Sit down, if you please.' He spoke harshly in French. I guessed that he was an educated Tunisian Arab who had been trained under French sponsorship and who for some reason was determined to put all Europeans in their places.

'Your name is Paul Temple?'

'Yes.'

'Your nationality?'

'British.'

'Your passport, please.'

I took my passport out and handed it to him. He turned the pages over suspiciously for several minutes then pushed it back towards me.

'What is the purpose of your visit to Tunis?'

'Pleasure, I suppose. What you call tourism.'

'I see. Did you come here for the purpose of meeting Patrick O'Halloran?'

'Certainly not. I had no idea—'

'But you had an appointment to meet him in the American Bar of this hotel at six this evening?'

'No. He followed us in—'

'How long has this Patrick O'Halloran been known to you? I looked at my watch.

'About two hours. I never set eyes on him before this evening—'

'You maintain that he is not a friend of yours? You were seen to engage in a very animated conversation with him.'

101

'I see you have been talking to Achmed. Why all these questions, *Commissaire*? Has O'Halloran picked someone's pocket?'

'Please not to jest with me, *Monsieur* Temple. This is a serious matter, and I warn you not to trifle with me. If you do not want to tell the truth and give me your full co-operation—'

'*Monsieur le Commissaire,*' I interrupted, 'I am ready to give you my full co-operation. Would it not be better if you explained to me just what the purpose of this interrogation is? What has O'Halloran done?'

Renouk fixed his dark eyes on me and studied my reactions closely.

'A body was found in the Arab quarter at half-past six this evening. It has been identified as that of Patrick O'Halloran. We believe that you are the last person who saw him alive.'

Chapter Six

STEVE and I did not eat a very hearty dinner that evening. Goodness knows we had both experienced our fair share of sudden and violent deaths. But the fate of Mr. O'Halloran shocked us unaccountably. We felt a genuine grief at the thought of that whiskyfied voice being permanently silenced.

'I had an instinct that he was connected with the spectacles in some way,' Steve said.

'Go easy, Steve. The fact that a man is killed in the streets of Tunis does not mean that he was involved in all this business.'

'Don't you think it's too much to be coincidence, Paul? Considering all that happened. Here's a man, whom you yourself took for a pick-pocket, who engineers a conversation with us and an hour later is found dead—'

'Actually, I agree with you, Steve.'

I took the oil and vinegar which the waiter had brought and began to mix a dressing for our lettuce.

'You remember how insistent he was about our visiting the House of Shoni?'

Steve suddenly reached for her handbag, which she had deposited on one of the empty chairs. We had both of us thought of the same thing at the same time. I suspended my salad operations while she reached her bag.

'Have you still got it?'

'Yes. Here it is.'

While Steve studied the card which Mr. O'Halloran had given her, I saw the vague outline of a drawing on the reverse side.

'Have a look on the other side, Steve.'

She turned the card over, then lifted her eyes to mine and silently handed it across the table. Crudely drawn on the back was a pair of thick-rimmed spectacles.

'This clinches it. Mr. O'Halloran himself may not have known what it was all about, but there's not much doubt that Zoltan Gupte belongs to the vast company of spectacle fanciers. I wonder whether we know him already under some other name?'

Steve and I ate our salad in silence. When the waiter came along, waving his huge menu, we both shook our heads.

'Just coffee for me, Paul. But don't let me stop you—'

'Let's go outside on the terrace. It's awfully close in here.'

'We're staying in the hotel,' I told the waiter as he pulled Steve's chair out of her way. 'Room number three seven two.'

'*Bien, monsieur. Merci, monsieur-dame.*'

We left him slapping the table with his serviette and wandered across the foyer towards the terrace which overlooked the hotel's small garden. It was an attractive place with crazy paving and rustic tables and chairs under coloured umbrellas. Now that it was dark, little coloured lights had been switched on among the trees. A three-man orchestra was playing sultry music above a small marble square where nobody was dancing yet.

We were picking and choosing among the tables when a voice from behind us spoke.

'Well, hallo there!'

Even as we turned round I was thinking that Audry Bryce's previous engagement had not lasted long. If all her dates were as abbreviated as this evening's, it was small wonder she was still *Miss*.

She was sitting on one of those very low swinging garden seats. Her long, well-shaped legs were crossed in an elegant V. They seemed to glow invitingly in the gloom.

'Why don't you come and join me?' she called out.

'Thank you. We'd love to,' Steve said.

We moved towards the table, and the next few minutes were taken up with arranging seats and swapping politenesses. Audry Bryce already had her coffee, so I ordered two more cups for Steve and me and liqueurs for all three of us.

'You're feeling quite better now, Mrs. Temple?'

'Much better, thank you. We had a wonderful ride in a cab through the most interesting parts of Tunis—'

'Those old cabs! They are quaint, don't you find? Personally I think Tunis is absolutely fascinating. I only came here for a week in the first place, and I've stayed a month already. It's such an extraordinary mixture; you know – the East hand in hand with the West, all those cute little shops in the Arab quarter. You know that Tunis is famous for perfumes? They tell me that there are secrets in the manufacture of perfumes which are kept in one family and only handed by word of mouth from father to son. And they make the most divine leather goods. Morocco leather, I suppose you call it. The cutest little slippers.'

'We rather wanted to buy some things of that kind while we are here,' I cut in. 'We were recommended a place in the Rue de Mirabar. I wonder if you know it? It's called the House of Shoni.'

Audry Bryce's eyes had sharpened. She listened to me attentively, then made a throwing gesture towards me with one hand.

'The House of Shoni,' she said disparagingly. 'No, I don't know it, and I'd advise you against going there. You've been talking to that revolting little Irishman who pesters all the new guests who come here – what's his name – O'Harrigan or something.'

'O'Halloran.'

'That's him. O'Halloran.' She switched her attention to Steve. 'Don't you pay any attention to him, Mrs. Temple. He's just a little tout who's after your money. For a start he drinks too much. Why the other morning at nine a.m. he was positively reeking with whisky. Now, I don't know about you, but if there's one thing I don't care for it's—'

'He was murdered earlier this evening,' I said. 'The police were here just before dinner, making enquiries. I'm surprised they didn't want to talk to you.'

Audry Bryce's flow was cut off in mid-stream. For a moment her guard dropped and her face was that of a rather stupid, frightened woman.

'Murdered? But that's impossible!'

'Why impossible? Tunis is a pretty violent place. We know that all too well, don't we, Steve?'

Steve smiled at me feebly. I was watching Audry Bryce as she struggled to recover herself.

'What I mean to say is it's impossible to imagine anyone wanting to murder such an insignificant person. I mean the motive could hardly be robbery, could it?'

'I shouldn't have thought so. Unless, of course, O'Halloran was a thief who had stolen something of value and was himself attacked and robbed before he could dispose of it.'

The American girl's eyes widened with dismay as she heard my suggestion. She reached for her glass of Benedictine and took a quick gulp at it.

'This is terrible! What an evening it has been! First that brutal attack on Mrs. Temple, and now this poor O'Halloran person being murdered. I'm sure I won't be able to sleep a wink to-night.'

She had been gathering up her impedimenta as she spoke – an evening bag, a gauze shawl for her shoulders, a glossy-backed American novel.

'Now I must ask you to excuse me. I promised a friend I would telephone him before ten o'clock.'

I stood while she made her departure, then sat down on the swinging seat beside Steve.

I felt for matches and lit up one of the small cigars I had bought during our tour that afternoon. Steve watched the first smoke-ring curl up into the midnight blue darkness.

'You were very hard on Miss Bryce, Paul. I think you frightened her away.'

'Miss Bryce is as transparent as a bottle of Vichy water. If she's an innocent American tourist you and I are Don Quixote and Sancho Panza.'

'What do you think she's up to?'

'As Sherlock Holmes said: "I haven't a clue." We'll find out in time. Do you feel like dancing? There are some people on the floor now.'

'No. Let's go on sitting here.' Steve put her arm through mine. 'You enjoy your cigar. I like watching the smoke-rings go up.'

On our way up to bed I called at the reception desk and asked for the Night Manager. He came out from his office, pulling a serviette from inside the front of his collar. I knew that we had interrupted his dinner.

'I just wanted to ask you one thing. How long has Miss Bryce been staying here?'

'The American lady? Fifteen days, *monsieur*. She is a friend to you, is it not?'

I agreed vaguely that she was, and the Night Manager beamed.

'You like your room, *monsieur?*'

'Yes, it's very nice.'

'Miss Bryce said you would admire the view. It was difficult for me to give you the room next to her, but she has been very generous to the staff, so we—'

'She asked you to put us in that room?'

'*Mais oui, monsieur.* We always try to oblige our guests.'

'Yes, it is most kind of you. Thank you very much. *Bonne nuit.*'

'Good night, mister. Good night, lady. Good repose.'

As we waited for the lift I said to Steve: 'Obviously he likes plenty of garlic in his mash.'

The light glowed to show that the lift was on our floor. The automatic doors rumbled across and we stepped into the lift. It was, I thought, as private a place for a conversation as one could find – or for a murder.

'What are you thinking about, Paul?'

I said: 'Have you noticed that since we arrived in Tunis there has been no sign of either Tony Wyse or Simone Lalange?'

'Are you pining for her?'

'No. I was just wondering whether their tour of duty finished when we touched down at El Aouina and their places were taken by Pat O'Halloran and Audry Bryce.'

*

108

The walls of the hotel had maintained the heat of the day and the atmosphere inside our bedroom was stiflingly hot. Even though we threw off all the bedclothes it was difficult to sleep. Very fresh in our minds, too, was the thought of Mr. O'Halloran and that disturbing revelation of violence in the Arab quarter. I supposed we dozed off every now and then, but the hours passed with maddening slowness.

At about three o'clock I heard Steve slip furtively out of bed and move towards the balcony in search of a breath of air. In a minute she was back, shaking me by the shoulder.

'Wake up, Paul,' she whispered. 'There's something going on in the next room – Audry Bryce's.'

There was no need for me to force myself into wakefulness. I had never been properly asleep.

'What sort of thing? Not another strangling match, for Timothy's sake!'

'No. Voices. There's a man in with her.'

'Oh, Steve,' I expostulated, and lay down again.

'No, Paul. Be serious. Come and listen.'

'All right. But you stay in here out of the way.'

Steve was reluctant to do as I asked, but I persuaded her to keep in the darkness while I went out cautiously on to the moonlit balcony. The windows of the adjoining room were open, and I could see the light streaming out. I was able to hear the mumble of voices, a man's and a woman's, but it was impossible to determine what they were saying. I guessed from their intonation that they were speaking in English.

The voices stopped after a few minutes. I was wondering whether I dared to climb the wall on to the other balcony when a woman's shadow fell across the rectangle of light: Audry Bryce's voice, though pitched low, sounded only a few feet away.

'All the same, you should have warned me that he had been killed. Suppose I had given myself away? All the good work Sam and I did earlier this evening would have been thrown away.'

The shadow was suddenly duplicated, and I could picture the man standing behind her, with his hands on her shoulders.

'How could I tell you, *chérie,* when I did not know about it myself? And I am sure you did not give yourself away. You are too clever for that. Come away from the window now. We do not want to disturb our neighbours, do we?'

The shadows moved back, and at the same time I hoisted myself on to the wall and dropped quietly down on the other side. They were well inside the room now, but by putting my ear to the crack of the door just beside the hinge I could hear something of what was said.

The man was speaking again.

'—I never really expected that they would be so foolish as to leave them in the bedroom. Have you any idea which of the two carries them?'

'Temple, I am sure. He does not wear glasses himself, but there is a slight bulge in his breast pocket which is not accounted for by his handkerchief.'

'Mmm. It is what I thought. If only he were not so well known to the police. Still, our time will come. We shall find a way. Only there is not so much time.'

'They are bound to be suspicious. That fool Leyland! To be caught in the room like that. He must have heard the key in the lock. You must get rid of him, Pierre. He is a terrible bungler.'

'Sam has his uses,' Pierre said. 'He may be stupid but he's trustworthy. He has not the brains to double-cross me, and for that I value him.'

110

'As long as I don't have to do any more jobs with him—'

'You won't. Your job is to keep friendly with the Temples.'

'Oh, I'm good at being friendly, you should know that, Pierre.'

Audry Bryce's voice had changed. 'You don't have to go for a while yet, do you, honey? We have so few chances of being alone together.'

'No, I don't have to go yet.' Pierre's voice had become husky. I heard a rustle of silk and the sudden subsidence of divan springs. I knew there was going to be nothing more in that conversation for my ears.

Steve was agog when I rejoined her.

'Well, could you hear anything?' she whispered. 'Did you recognize the voices?'

'Audry Bryce, of course, though she sounded a good deal less like the stock edition of an American tourist. I'll know the other voice to my dying day. It was Rostand.'

'Rostand! So he's in Tunis. Could you hear what they were saying?'

I closed our windows gently so that we could talk above a whisper without danger of ourselves being overheard. Then I repeated the conversation which had taken place in the next room.

'Thanks to Audry Bryce's forethought we have acquired some useful information.'

'Though I suppose her real reason for wanting us in the room next door to her was so that they could search it, and if that didn't work scrape an acquaintance with us. What was the particular bit of information you were so pleased about, Paul?'

'Well, we've confirmed that the spectacles themselves are what everyone is after, though we really knew that all along. What we now know for certain is that more than one gang is interested in them. Rostand and his troupe did not know about O'Halloran and what he was up to. I suspected this all along. It's the only explanation for all the killings there have been.'

'I think I see what you mean. Whenever one of the greyhounds gets too close the others eat him up.'

'That's about it.'

'What happens when there's only one greyhound left?'

'It'll be some time before that happens. There are an awful lot of greyhounds in this race.'

'There seem to be, don't there? All after a perfectly ordinary pair of spectacles. That's what's so fantastic about the whole thing. I wish you'd hurry up and find out why, Paul.'

Steve was gazing at me with a rapt, intent expression as if I were a slot-machine into which she had put her sixpence and which was expected to disgorge a card telling her fortune. I found myself laughing at her.

'Usually it's quite a different story; you're begging me to give the case up and stay out of trouble.'

'I know. But this time I confess I'm so curious that I can hardly bear it. And besides, I don't have a feeling that anything awful is going to happen to you.'

After our disturbed night we slept late the following morning. When we woke I rang down for breakfast to be brought up to our room. I shaved and took a cold shower while waiting for it to arrive. Steve ate her *croissants* and drank her coffee in bed, wriggling about in luxurious sleepiness and yawning her head off. It was obvious that she would not be mobile for some considerable time, so I decided to go round to the bank on my own. I made a little parcel of the spectacles and inserted it in an envelope before replacing it in my breast pocket. I lowered and bolted the wooden sun-blind and made Steve get out of bed to lock the door on the inside when I left.

'Don't open up for anyone,' I said. 'I shan't be long – not more than half an hour.'

As things turned out it took me rather longer than that to complete my errand. On my way to the Tunis branch of Lloyds Bank my attention was arrested by an optician's window display. I had taken certain precautions to make sure that I discarded anyone who might have felt inclined to follow me, so I did not hesitate before going inside.

A tall, cadaverous man with sparse white hair was crouching over a table in a small glass-walled compartment, examining something through an eye-glass fixed in one eye. He straightened up painfully and walked with tiny steps to the other side of the counter.

'I want to buy a case for a pair of glasses,' I said.

'Eye-test?' he asked, screwing up his eyes. I realized he must be very deaf. I came to a sudden and unexpected decision.

'Yes, please,' I said more loudly.

He looked happier and began to fuss round towards a little cubicle with all the familiar paraphernalia of eye-testing.

'If you will come this way, please, sir.'

Lights were switched on and a dark curtain drawn across to shield us from the outside world. We went through the usual routine of reading the rows of letters on the printed card. Then he made me look at the bright red spot and the two parallel lines that want so terribly badly to be joined together. I shut one eye and we gazed at each other like loving Cyclops for several seconds.

'Yes,' he told me seriously when the ritual was over. 'You ought to be wearing spectacles.'

'I was afraid you'd tell me that,' I said sadly. Fortunately for me I've enjoyed perfect sight all my life.

'It will take several days to make them up. Can you call back, shall we say, on Tuesday?'

'I'm afraid not. I'm just passing through Tunis, but I was especially recommended to consult you. If you'd just let me have the prescription.'

It took a few moments for that to sink in, but he was pleased at this suggestion of world fame and consented to write a series of figures on a sheet of headed notepaper. He handed it to me with a pinched little smile.

'How much do I owe you?'

'Two thousand francs.'

'And cheap at the price,' I told him. I meant it too. He was happy enough about the whole thing to lead me to the door and bow me out.

When I entered the offices of Lloyds Bank I felt as if the whole of Tunis were an illusion which ceased to have effect the moment I passed through these portals. The place had an indefinable English aura about it, and reminded me irresistibly of my own branch in London. The chummy, smiling man in correct grey suiting behind the counter gave me a tremendous sense of security, and when I explained that I was a customer of Lloyds he readily agreed to place my package in the strong-room.

I felt considerably less vulnerable when I emerged into the street again. That faint bulge in my breast pocket had seemed as dangerous as a time-bomb liable to blow up at any moment.

I hailed a taxi to take me back to the hotel. I had told Steve that I would only be half an hour, and already an hour had passed since I left her. Going through the hotel *foyer* I

114

kept my eyes open, but there was no sign of Audry Bryce or anyone even remotely resembling the so-called Colonel Rostand. I had to share the lift with a disquieting unveiled girl in Arab dress, who bore tattooed signs on her brow and cheeks. She was probably not more than fifteen, but as fully developed as a European woman of twenty, and to judge by her expression a good deal more worldly wise. She gazed at me with a kind of anticipatory relish. I was very relieved when the lift doors sighed open at the third floor.

There was no answer to my knock on the door of room number three seven two. I turned the handle and it opened.

'Steve!'

No answer from the bathroom. Then I saw a sheet of paper on the floor just inside the door.

'Got tired of waiting. Have gone to buy cute morocco leather slippers. Meet you for coffee on the hotel terrace at eleven.
    S.'

'Not at all wise,' I muttered to myself. I glanced at my watch. It was three minutes to eleven.

I closed the door and left the key rattling on the inside. If anyone wanted to search the room it would be more convenient for all concerned if they did not have to force the lock.

Something made me knock on Audry Bryce's door as I went past. No one answered. Rather than face the lift again I ran down the stairs to the hotel *foyer*.

'Have you seen my wife come in yet?' I asked the reception clerk.

'No, *monsieur*. She has not come back yet.'

'You saw her go out, then?'

'Yes, *monsieur*. About twenty minutes ago.'

'She was alone?'

'Yes, *monsieur.*'

A heavy brief case was deposited with a clatter on the counter close beside me. A voice spoke in stiff and guttural French.

'You have a reservation for me, I think. The name is Schultz.'

I turned round and saw the blond features and athletic form of the proprietor of the El Passaro Club.

'Hallo,' I said in English. 'You seem to get around.'

'*Pardon, monsieur?*'

'Perhaps you don't remember me. I met you at your club the other evening.'

'Excuse me, sir,' the German said. 'I have so many customers. It is impossible to remember them all.'

'You don't remember the police inspector who was trying to trace your friend Colonel Rostand?'

'Ah, yes, sir. I remember you now. You I think were also trying to find someone. A Mister Constantin. Were you successful?'

'No,' I said. 'I'm afraid I did not find him that evening, and have not seen him since. A pity, because I had hoped we might do some profitable business together.'

Schultz nodded curtly, turning his head towards the clerk.

'Excuse me, please. It has been nice to meet you again.'

'You have a place here too, haven't you?' I persisted. 'I'd like to take my wife there. What's it called?'

"It's called *Le Trou du Diable*. The Devil's Hole, sir. It is out at Sidi bou Saïd.'

'Then I may see you there.'

Schultz shrugged non-committally and dropped me like a soiled handkerchief.

Not many people were using the hotel terrace at that time of day, but it was shady and pleasant. Steve had not yet arrived. I picked a table from which I could see the door she would come out by. I ordered a black coffee and a glass of iced water, then settled down to enjoy the second cigarette of the day.

I was stubbing it out when a patch of brilliant colour drew my eyes to the hotel doorway. Simone Lalange was standing there, poised like a ballerina as she looked around. She was wearing a scarlet shirt and a swinging white skirt. Her arms and shoulders were a deep bronzed colour. She saw me, gave a little wave, and began to move towards me with graceful elegance. Her waist was tiny and her skirt swayed to the movement of her hips.

I stood up as, uninvited, she sank into a chair beside mine.

'What a pleasure to encounter you again!' she exclaimed with apparent sincerity. 'Mrs. Temple is not with you?'

'I was just waiting for her. She's gone to do some shopping. May I offer you something to drink? Coffee or an *apéritif*?'

She frowned and pouted her lips.

'Perhaps a juice of fruit. Orange, if they have it.'

I snapped my fingers at the waiter and gave the order. She refused my offer of a cigarette with a smile, and took the gold case from her handbag.

'I prefer to smoke mine.'

I watched her fit the cigarette into the holder and put it to her lips. I did not offer her a light. I wanted to see if Steve had been right about the initials on her book matches. The French girl lit her cigarette with concentrated attention, then threw the book of matches on the table. It fell with the initials S.L. facing towards me. I glanced up and caught her eyes fixed on me mockingly. She was indeed a very attractive woman and quite aware of it.

'You are enjoying your stay in Tunis, Mr. Temple?'

'Apart from one or two minor mishaps, very much, thank you. I'm surprised not to see Tony Wyse with you.'

'Oh, he?' Simone lifted one shoulder and began to swing her leg petulantly. 'He is a nice enough boy but one can have too much of him. I managed to give him the cold brush-off, as you say it.'

'He offered to show us all over Tunis, but we haven't seen him at all. Do you know where he is staying?'

'He told me he was going to the Hôtel Mimosa. I expect he is busy with business, and that is why you have not seen him.'

'We'll manage without him,' I said casually. 'We've been offered the services of another guide – a Mr. Patrick O'Halloran.'

Simone Lalange leant back to allow the waiter to pour out her fruit juice. She had not shown the slightest interest in my statement. Not even her long imitation eyelashes had flickered.

I said: 'I see Mr. Schultz has arrived in the hotel here. Perhaps you saw him as you came in?'

The two straws in the rapidly frosting glass were already between her lips. She looked up at me with innocent eyes.

'Mr. Schultz? Who is that? Do I know him?'

'He is the proprietor of the El Passaro Club. Perhaps you've forgotten our dance there?'

It was a remark which Steve would not have failed to hold against me. Simone looked at me sideways. She was very provocative, with her lips rounded to the shape of the straw and her throat moving slightly as she drank.

She leaned forward to put the half empty glass on the table.

'I have not forgotten that. I was asking myself if one day we might be able to dance together again. It was so short, was it not?'

'Simone,' I said, and hoped my voice did not sound too intense, 'that time when the lights went out. Was it you who took the spectacles from my pocket and hid them in my wife's bag?'

Simone's peal of laughter made all heads turn in our direction.

'You are still thinking about that? Why should I want to do a so stupid thing as that?'

'I don't know. I was hoping that perhaps you could tell me.'

'You think perhaps I try to make trouble between a man and his wife?'

'No. I don't think that.'

'Mr. Temple. Why do you keep looking at your watch. Are you so bored as that?'

'I'm sorry. It's just that my wife said she would meet me here at eleven and it's now after a quarter to twelve.'

'Well, a woman forgets about the time when she is shopping. I will try to keep you amused until she comes.'

Simone Lalange did keep me highly entertained for the next quarter of an hour. It is a pleasant sensation to be vamped by an attractive woman who is an expert at the game. In spite of my growing disquiet about Steve I could not help admiring her performance. In the end she gave me a wry grin, and began to get up.

'I have enjoyed our conversation. I think Mrs. Temple is a fortunate woman.'

'Why do you say that?'

'To have such an implacably faithful husband.'

I tried to indicate by my parting smile that I wished things could have been different. It was five past twelve when she disappeared into the hotel. Steve was an hour and five minutes overdue. She could be half an hour late, even three-quarters, but never so late as this.

119

I gave Simone a few moments' start then hurried into the hotel. I had a sudden idea that I knew where Steve's instinct might have taken her. At the reception desk I paused long enough to leave a message in case she came back while I was gone. She was to wait for me in our room. Then I ran out into the street and grabbed the taxi which was just depositing a fare at the hotel.

'Take me to the House of Shoni. It's at 227 Avenue de Mirabar.'

Chapter Seven

THE Rue de Mirabar was a long straggling street half in and half out of the Arab quarter. The House of Shoni stood on a corner where a narrow, noisome alley disappeared into the maze of tiny streets of which we had caught a glimpse during our coach ride the previous evening. It was a glorified junk *cum* antique shop, crammed with bric-à-brac picked up from everywhere between Timbuctoo and Stratford-upon-Avon. I told the driver to wait while I went to the glass door and peered inside, hoping against hope that I would see Steve's familiar face, animated by the fascination of knocking the price of an antique down by twenty per cent. But the shop was empty of customers. With a sinking heart I pushed open the door. Above my head a small bell gave vent to a hearty ping. Almost at once a bead curtain covering a doorway behind the shop was parted and the shopkeeper came through.

Zoltan Gupte, for it was he, was an anthropological puzzle. At first sight I put him down as one of the Jewish community which lives on such uneasy terms with the Arabs of North Africa. Then I wondered if he were not more of an Indian, with his brown skin and jet-black hair. Later on, when I had a chance to examine his police dossier I found out that

121

he was almost half-Turkish and spoke a dozen languages fluently. English was one of them. He shot me a look of intense astuteness and instantly decided on my nationality.

'Good morning, sir. Is there anything special I can show you?'

'As a matter of fact I came here to find my wife. Have you had a visit this morning from an English lady? I am afraid I don't know what she was wearing, but she's dark and she may have bought slippers.'

Zoltan Gupte was already shaking his head.

'I have had no English ladies this morning, sir. Perhaps she has not arrived yet. You would like to have a look round while you are waiting?'

There was something defensive about the shopkeeper's manner, as if he knew that these were only the opening thrusts in a duel.

I decided to come straight to the point. I took out my wallet and extracted from it the card which O'Halloran had given us. I turned it over, making sure that the shopkeeper saw the drawing on the back. Then I handed him the card.

'We were recommended to come here by a man who said he was a representative of yours. His name is written on the card.'

Zoltan Gupte took the card without surprise. He merely glanced at the drawing at the back then slipped the card into his jacket pocket.

'Is your name Temple?'

'Yes.'

He nodded, pursing his lips and studying my face carefully.

'Come this way, please. I have a friend of yours here.'

He led the way round behind the counter and held back the bead curtain for me to pass through. I am always reluctant to precede strange men through strange doorways. It's one of the easiest ways of having your skull cracked open. But

I was now far more concerned about Steve's safety than my own. I ducked through and found myself in a narrow corridor.

'It is the door opposite you at the end.'

I went ahead and opened the door. It revealed a sitting-room furnished with the most fabulous oriental luxury. The walls were hung with rare silks and damasks, the floor carpeted with Persian and Kairouan rugs. Brilliantly woven materials had been draped over the divans. There was an almost Victorian profusion of furniture, each piece a miracle of intricate workmanship. The air was heavy with the scent of joss-sticks.

The man who stood facing the door was utterly incongruous in this setting, but his good spirits were in no wise dampened.

'So there ye are at last! Sure, I'd almost given ye up as a bad job.'

It was several seconds before I found my voice. Behind me I heard Zoltan Gupte chuckle as he gently closed the door.

'O'Halloran! But I thought you were dead. The police told me you'd been murdered. In fact at one time I thought I was going to be accused of committing the crime.'

O'Halloran slapped his knee and almost doubled up with mirth.

'Bring the gentleman a glass, Shamus,' he said to Gupte when he recovered his breath. 'This calls for a celebration.'

Gupte opened a large cabinet which contained several rows of bottles and brought out a glass. The whisky bottle and soda syphon were already on the table within easy reach of Mr. O'Halloran. In the meantime I noted that the Irishman was now wearing a suit which fitted him passably well.

'You're thinkin' I'm a sight better dressed than when ye last saw me – is that it, Mr. Temple? If ever ye want to do the disappearin' trick yeself there's nothin' I recommend better

123

than bein' murdered. All ye have to do is find a corpse of the right size and colour and give him the lend of yer clothes and wallet. The police will do the rest, God bless 'em!'

'Say when, Mr. Temple,' Zoltan Gupte's quiet voice interrupted.

'Just a little whisky and plenty of soda, please,' I said, and turned back to O'Halloran.

'I suppose it's not hard to come by a corpse in the Arab quarter – judging by what we saw last night.'

'They're two a penny,' O'Halloran told me happily. 'And when I want to come back to life all I have to do is go to the police and tell 'em I was robbed.'

I was anxious to find out what had been O'Halloran's motive in making this complicated manœuvre, but there was something else I had to ask him first.

'O'Halloran, do you know anything about my wife's present whereabouts? I have good reason to believe she intended coming here this morning.'

'And how would I know anythin' about that seein' I haven't been out of this room since last evenin'! Has she been to the shop at all, Shamus?'

'I have already told Mr. Temple that his wife has not been here.'

'Perhaps she'll turn up later on,' O'Halloran said, dismissing the matter. 'Why don't ye take the weight off your feet? I think ye're entitled to an explanation from me.'

Zoltan Gupte pushed a chair forward and I sat down. He offered me a cigarette from an ornately worked silver box, but this I declined.

'The reason why I wanted ye to come here, Mr. Temple, was because there's something ye have got which I'd like ye to hand over to me without anyone else's knowledge.'

'Oh, and what is that?'

'I think ye know already. It's a pair of spectacles belongin' to a Mr. David Foster.'

'I see.'

O'Halloran was frank at any rate.

'Have ye got them with ye?'

'I'm afraid I haven't, Mr. O'Halloran.'

'But they're still in your possession?'

'I know where they are and no one else can get them. Why are you so interested in them?'

'All I want to do is hand them over to their rightful owner.'

O'Halloran had sat down on the edge of a chair facing me, his glass of whisky cradled between the palms of his hands. Zoltan Gupte was still standing watchfully by the door.

'Why doesn't this Mr. David Foster approach me about the glasses himself?'

'Ah!' O'Halloran exclaimed. 'Now that's the crux of the whole matter! Ye're wonderin' why ye've never set eyes on Foster, wonderin' why he didn't meet ye at the airport – is that it?'

'Yes. I have been wondering about that.'

'Well, the explanation's a simple one. Foster is a very close friend of mine, so I can tell ye all about it. The fact is, he's wanted by the police.'

O'Halloran made the announcement in an awed voice, as if this was an adequate explanation for the whole thing. He must have seen my sceptical look, for he rattled on.

'Yes, wanted by the police he is, the poor fellow, and for a crime he didn't commit too. You can imagine what it's like, Mr. Temple, especially for a man that's as active as he is, to be confined to the house and never able to put a nose outside for fear the police'll grab him. He can pass the time in readin', ye'll say, to improve his mind. But how can he read when he hasn't his glasses with him? Will ye answer me that, now. Sure he's as blind as a bat without 'em. It's a pitiful sight, I'm tellin' ye, in sowl.'

Mr. O'Halloran was a great deal more carried away by his recital than I was. There were genuine tears in his eyes. I finished my whisky and stood up.

'You'll have to do better than that, Mr. O'Halloran. I just don't believe a word you say.'

If looks could be killers, Mr. O'Halloran's glance would have dropped me dead in my tracks.

'Bah! Some people have no decent feelin's in them.'

Zoltan Gupte came smoothly forward. He had been watching all this with an amused smile.

'Pat likes his little joke, Mr. Temple. I think on the whole we understand each other very well. You say you have not got the spectacles with you?'

'I'd hardly be likely to, since they've been valued at ten thousand pounds, would I?'

O'Halloran jumped to his feet, sending his empty glass splintering to the floor.

'Ten thousand pounds? Where do ye get this idea from?'

'That was the offer made to me by a *Monsieur* Constantin.'

O'Halloran and Zoltan Gupte exchanged a glance.

'You know him, then?' I asked.

'I know of him,' Zoltan Gupte admitted cautiously.

'Did you know that he had been murdered – and I mean really murdered, not like our friend O'Halloran here. I've seen his body.'

'I did not know this.' The only change in Zoltan Gupte's manner was that he began to breathe a little faster and I saw tiny beads of sweat break out on his forehead.

'When did it happen?'

'In Algiers, the night before last.'

'Do the police know who committed this crime?'

'They do. It was a man known as Colonel Rostand, aided and abetted by an accomplice of his called Sam Leyland.'

'Rostand, did you say? What was the other name?'

'It's an English name. Leyland. You don't know him?'

'No,' Zoltan Gupte shook his head. 'Nor this Colonel Rostand. He is French?'

'Maybe French. Maybe American. He speaks both languages.' The shopkeeper turned to O'Halloran.

'Do these names mean anything to you, Pat?'

O'Halloran shook his head. He was still sulking. Zoltan Gupte pondered for a moment. I was sure he was about to make some suggestion, so I waited. Sure enough it came.

'If we were to present you to the real David Foster, Mr. Temple, I take it that you would be prepared to hand the glasses over to him. What would your price be?'

'Why should I have a price? If he can prove his identity he can have his glasses.'

'Then the sooner we can arrange this the better.' Zoltan Gupte was rubbing his hands, glancing suggestively at O'Halloran. The bell in the shop sounded at that moment. Gupte excused himself and went to attend to whoever it was.

'What about this evenin', Temple?' O'Halloran suggested. 'Are ye free?'

'I'd rather you made it before then.'

'That's impossible, I'm afraid. We'll have to wait till it's dark or very nearly.'

'That means about seven o'clock. Where shall I meet you?'

O'Halloran thought for a moment. 'Ye know Khérédin?'

'That's the kind of bracelet of land that curves round and encloses the inner bay of Tunis?'

'That's right. It's where the ships and docks are. Now there's a fellow called Durant has a boatyard out there. His house is beside a place called the Hôtel du Port. I'll meet you there at seven o'clock this evenin', without fail.'

Zoltan Gupte had pushed open the door again.

'It is your taxi-driver, Mr. Temple. He does not know whether to wait any longer.'

'Tell him I'll be out in a moment. Now this is on the level, O'Halloran? No more disappearing tricks?'

'Cross me heart and hope to die. Oh, and Temple . . .'

I stopped in the doorway and glanced back to find him grinning at me.

'You won't let on to the police that I'm not murdered after all. They're no friends of mine and I like to see them makin' jack-asses of themselves.'

'Don't you worry. As far as I'm concerned you're a dead duck.'

As I walked up the corridor I could hear his delighted laughter through the closed door.

It was a quarter to two when I entered the Hôtel François Premier again. Four hours had passed since I had last set eyes on Steve. A glance towards the dining-room showed me that it was already almost empty. People lunch early in Tunis.

The clerk at the reception desk gave me an amused look when he saw me approaching him with anxious face. Clearly he had classified me as a husband who was worried in case his wife went off with another man.

'Has Mrs. Temple come in?'

'No, *monsieur.*'

'You're absolutely sure?'

'Not through the *foyer*, *monsieur*. I told the *chasseurs* to keep a watch for her.'

'And there has been no message?'

'Yes. *Le Commissaire* Renouk telephoned. You are to put yourself in touch with him as soon as you return.'

'But no message from Mrs. Temple?'

The clerk's patience was rapidly dwindling.

'Nothing from Mrs. Temple, *monsieur*. Nothing at all.'

'Perhaps she's in our room,' I said, and began to turn away.

He called after me as I hurried towards the lift. 'Your key, *monsieur*.'

'But I left it in the door.'

'The *femme de chambre* brought it down when she had done your room, *monsieur*.'

He handed me the key, and although this confirmed that Steve had not come back, I went up to number three hundred and seventy-two. As I had expected, the bed had been made, the floor swept, and all our clothes neatly put away. That left little chance of finding out whether Steve had left the room voluntarily. Even the scrap of paper with her message had been tidied away. I thought I was unlikely to have been deceived by her hand-writing, although there was one person who could have faked the message about the cute slippers. On the whole I felt inclined to believe that the note had been genuine. She had gone out of the hotel of her own accord, and whatever had happened to her had taken place in the street.

The room was terribly empty with only me in it. I almost gave way to despair when my eye fell on the dressing-table with all Steve's familiar things on it. If I hadn't gone out and left her alone—

I checked that way of thinking abruptly. To start blaming myself would not undo the harm. Now more than ever was a time for clear thinking. I had little stomach for food, but I knew that I had to make myself eat something. Very heavy calls might be made on both my mental and physical resources, and I could not meet them with an empty stomach. I went down to the now virtually deserted dining-room. Our waiter of the evening before concealed any impatience he might have felt and took my order for an omelette. It was all I could bring myself to tackle.

While waiting for the food to come I tried to put my thoughts in order. It was, of course, just possible that Steve had met with an accident or been taken suddenly ill. Later I would have to go through the disheartening business of checking the hospitals and police-stations. But I could not seriously bring myself to believe that. Her passport was in her handbag, and by now the authorities would have traced her back to the hotel. The obvious explanation was that she had been taken as a hostage to persuade me to part with the spectacles. Then why had I received no threatening message? I now wryly remembered my own remark to Steve about leaving Mr. O'Halloran to cook. I had certainly been put on hot bricks myself.

Who had organized the abduction of Steve? I sensed that Zoltan Gupte and O'Halloran knew nothing about it. That still left a good many other possibilities. I found them falling into groups in my mind. Rostand, Leyland and Audry Bryce formed one obvious trio. Leyland had already made one attack on Steve, and I knew how much violence Rostand was capable of. It seemed likely that if that group decided to abduct Steve they would have used Audry Bryce as a decoy, and surely Steve would have been suspicious of any approach by her.

Then there were Simone Lalange and Tony Wyse. The latter had kept well out of sight, and I had suspected all along that he was up to no good. The French girl had approached me that morning with what had appeared to be a calculated motive. By then Steve must have been in the bag. Why had Simone Lalange not opened the bargaining?

Lastly there was Schultz, whose arrival in the hotel almost coincided with Steve's disappearance. Obviously business must bring him regularly to Tunis, but why should he have to stay in a hotel when he had his own place out at Sidi bou Saïd? This surely meant that he belonged with Rostand's group, and had registered at the hotel to cover a meeting with the bogus colonel – probably in Audry Bryce's room.

Whoever had taken Steve, the shape of things was clear. I held the spectacles, they held the thing in the world which I valued most. Sooner or later they would approach me with a suggestion that we should make an exchange. This was the thought I must keep uppermost in my mind during the coming hours. As long as I had the spectacles, Steve was unlikely to be harmed. And since the way to Steve was via a solution of the mystery, I must continue to explore every avenue that offered itself.

I must resist the temptation to rush out into the street and start questioning the taxi-drivers and shop-keepers. That would only lead me into a blind alley.

I had eaten the omelette without noticing. The glass of wine which the waiter had poured out for me remained untouched. I decided to leave it and drank a glass of water instead. I was the last guest to leave the dining-room.

As I waited for the lift I could feel the desk clerk's eyes on my back. It reminded me that I was under orders to ring Renouk. Well, I could do that later.

There was no one in the corridor outside our room when I knocked hard on Audry Bryce's door. Still no reply. I went into our own room, locked the door and marched through to the balcony. Anyone who cared to look up from the street would have seen me climbing the dividing wall and entering the neighbouring room. It contained a single bed and had been left as tidy as our own. I bolted the door on the inside and then went systematically through Audry Bryce's possessions. She had obviously been well trained. There was not a single paper in her room. The only interesting thing I discovered was that most of her clothes had been bought in Paris, and that the tailor who had made her suit had obligingly written a name in the blank space on the trade label: *Mrs. Audry Leather*.

I unbolted the door before returning to my own room the way I had come. I sat on the bed, picked up the receiver and asked the hotel operator to put me through to the *Commissariat Central de Police*, *Commissaire* Renouk's office. I laid the instrument on my knee and lit a cigarette. Presently a male voice crackled against my leg. I picked up the receiver.

'I want to speak to *Commissaire* Renouk, please. My name is Temple.'

'*Monsieur le Commissaire* is not here, *monsieur*. He is gone to lunch some time ago.'

'Is he not back yet?' My watch said a quarter to three. Then I remembered the sacrosanct siesta. 'What time do you expect him?'

'Four o'clock, *monsieur* – maybe.'

'I suppose he leaves you his telephone number in case of an urgent message?'

'Well, yes, *monsieur* – but—'

'Then ring him at once and tell him that Mr. Temple will meet him in his office at three o'clock. Have you got that?'

'I cannot do that, *monsieur* . . .' The police clerk began to stammer.

132

'You'd better,' I told him, and slammed the receiver down.

A sleek, well-polished Citroen, with a driver at the wheel, was standing outside Police Headquarters when I drove up in my taxi. It was just on three. A uniformed policeman intercepted me in the hall.

'You are Mr. Temple?'

'Yes. I've come to see *le Commissaire* Renouk.'

'*Monsieur le Commissaire* has sent his car. If you will mount the driver will take you to him.'

'That's very considerate of him. Thank you.'

The police Citroen took me at terrifying speed through the streets and deposited me at the steps of a villa which stood in its own small garden in the northern suburb of Tunis. At the sound of the car an Arab man-servant in a white coat opened the door and gave a friendly nod to my driver.

'*Monsieur le Commissaire* is awaiting you,' he informed me, and opened a door leading off the hall.

All the sunshades had been drawn, and when I entered this room after the brilliant sunlight I was as blind as a cinema-goer who comes in half-way through the film. I seemed to be swimming through a dense cloud of cigar smoke. Gradually the objects in the room became clear to me, among them Renouk.

He was taking his siesta seriously. Wearing a dressing-gown with his shirt collar loosened, he was reclining on a divan. I noticed a small liqueur glass at his elbow. He did not get up, but waved me to a chair.

'Sit down, sit down, Mr. Temple. I have been trying to get in touch with you. You will take a *digestif* – no? A cigar then. Yes, please smoke a cigarette if you prefer that.'

Something had happened to make Renouk more favourably disposed towards me. I soon learnt what it was.

'Since we last met I have had some messages from my colleagues in Algiers, Nice and Paris. I have also been in contact with Interpol in Paris.'

'I see. Then you know all about this curious business my wife and I have been unwittingly caught up in.'

'Well, it would be untrue to say I know all about it. But I know enough to be able to tell you that it is a very grave case. Very grave indeed. Tremendous stakes are involved, and you and your wife may be in very great danger.'

'You don't have to tell me that. My wife left the hotel between ten and eleven this morning and has not been seen since. It's my belief that she has been kidnapped.'

Renouk was startled enough to allow the long ash he was cultivating on his cigar to fall to the carpet. His jet-black eyebrows rose an inch.

'Kidnapped? You have had threatening messages?'

'Not so far. I was going to ask you if you would arrange for the hospitals to be checked – just in case . . .'

'I will do that,' Renouk said impatiently. 'Though I am convinced it will yield no result. I had been expecting that something like this would happen.'

He struggled to his feet, pulling his dressing-gown cord tighter round the place where his waist might have been had he indulged in less gastronomic midday meals.

'Now I understand from these reports that you have in your possession a pair of spectacles which seems to have some peculiar significance—'

'It's true that we've experienced nothing but trouble since they were handed to us. But both your colleagues in Nice and Algiers seemed convinced that these spectacles can have no special significance.'

'That view has been revised,' Renouk snapped. 'It is desired to make a more detailed examination of the spectacles, and I ask you to hand them over to me now.'

'I'm afraid I have not got them with me,' I said for the second time that day.

'Then perhaps you would be kind enough to fetch them. My driver will take you back to your hotel.'

'They're not at the hotel,' I began, then stopped. I had suddenly seen Renouk as a potential threat. My whole system of orientation had changed since eleven o'clock that morning. If I allowed the glasses to go out of my possession I would have nothing with which to barter for Steve's life and safety. And that had become for me the most important thing in the world.

I said: 'They were stolen from me this morning.'

'Stolen!' Renouk echoed furiously. 'Why did you allow such a thing to happen?'

'Well,' I pointed out, 'the police had assured me that these spectacles could have nothing to do with the murders, so naturally I took their word for it. I think a common pick-pocket must have removed them from me as I was going through a crowded street this morning.'

Renouk uttered an oath in Arabic and regarded me with exasperation.

'This is a serious development, *Monsieur* Temple. You are sure you are telling me the truth?'

'Why should I try to deceive you, *Monsieur le Commissaire*? I rely on your help to find my wife.'

'That is so,' the *Commissaire* agreed. 'We must go to Headquarters at once. You will give me as much informa-tion as you can while we are in the car. Excuse me while I go and put on my uniform.'

At Police Headquarters Renouk put a man on to checking all the hospitals and police-stations in Tunis. While I was waiting I had an opportunity of watching the *Commissaire* in action. He gave a great many orders and shouted his instructions very loudly at his subordinates, but I did not feel that he had a firm grip of the case. I was glad that I had not told him too much in the car. This was a situation which needed handling with velvet gloves.

The enquiries at the hospitals and police-stations produced a nil result.

'But do not worry, *Monsieur* Temple. If you will give me a description of your wife I will guarantee that every policeman and detective in Tunis will be on the watch for her. Who knows, it may jog a memory in some of my men's minds. If you have a photograph that would be even better.'

Luckily I had a very good snapshot of Steve in my wallet, taken from close up. I handed it to Renouk, who examined it with interest and then looked up at me.

'I can understand your disquiet, *monsieur*. You have a very attractive wife.'

I did not like to be away from the hotel for too long at a time. It was the most obvious place for anyone to try and contact me. Renouk was kind enough to send me back in his own car. He told me again not to worry, and I knew that only by keeping a clear head would I be of any use to Steve.

My supercilious friend at the reception desk had been relieved by another clerk when I got back, but the new man gave me the same answer. No messages. I controlled an impulse to pick up one of the huge ornamental vases and smash it against one of the shiny marble pillars. This was a war of nerves. Steve's kidnappers intended to work me up to a state of dithering suspense. It was quite possible that they had someone watching me, and I would only play into their hands if I gave any indication that my nerve was going.

'—there was only this cable for you from Paris, *monsieur.*'

I realized that the desk clerk was still talking to me, handing me an envelope across the counter.

I began to rip the cable open. This could be it: but why from Paris? I was glad to see that my hands were quite steady as I unfolded the slip of paper. The message had been handed in at two p.m. by Paris time.

'Arriving Tunis late to-night. Will contact you at hotel. Forbes.'

I stared across the hotel *foyer* in a daze. What was bringing my old friend from Scotland Yard to Tunis at this very psychological moment? He had disappeared from London some weeks before, and Steve and I half believed the story that his health had broken down and he had been ordered away for a rest cure. But if that were so, why was he posting to Tunis in such a hurry and how on earth did he know that we were staying at the Hôtel François Premier? Well, I'd know the answer that night, and this cable did mean one thing: I would have an ally in this terribly hostile and mystifying city.

'Not bad news, I hope?'

Audry Bryce. Luckily I had folded the cable up so she had had no chance of reading it over my shoulder. I turned and greeted her with a smile as open and frank as her own.

'No, thank you. Just a message from an old friend of mine at Scotland Yard.'

She rode that one, rather as a boxer rides a punch he has seen coming.

'Mrs. Temple is not around?'

I thought the phrasing of the question was rather false, as if she knew the answer.

'No, she's gone shopping. You know how women sometimes lose count of time. Why don't you join me for tea? I feel the need of company.'

'That's very kind of you, Mr. Temple. I'd just love to do that.'

She had fallen easily into her role as a dumb American tourist. We strolled out to the terrace like a couple of long lost friends gaily swapping trivialities. When the tea came I asked her if she would be 'mother', and we giggled together at the old joke.

'By the way,' I said, 'how's Pierre? I'm surprised he's not with you.'

The lid of the teapot fell with a crash on to my cup, knocked it over and sent tea sloshing all over the table. A damned fool of a waiter came hurtling forward and sacrificed his snow-white serviette to saving her skirt. It gave her a few moments cover to regain her composure.

'Who's this Pierre?' she asked me when the *status quo* had been restored. 'I don't seem to recall anyone of that name.'

'My mistake. I probably mistook him for someone else of the same name – or vice versa.'

'What's that again?'

'The same person with another name,' I said, and smiled brightly at her again.

'That's double talk,' she told me, but without conviction.

I took a sip of tea. It was weak and bleak, but I did not mind much. I was beginning to understand why cats find a peculiar fascination in playing with mice.

'We were interested in your tip about the slippers, Miss Bryce.'

'Oh, good. Did you manage to find the sort of thing you wanted?'

'I think so. I imagine that's very much your speciality.'

Her cup was half-way to her lips. It stopped there.

'My speciality? I don't get this.'

'Anything to do with – leather.'

She was worried now and on the defensive. She did not spill her tea this time, but the cup went down on to the saucer with an unhealthy crash. She began to become very busy about lighting a cigarette.

'This Pierre I was mentioning,' I said casually. 'Of course, I realize you don't know him, but it's an interesting story. He has been engaging in what you and I might call a rather shady business, and the police have been watching him for a very long time. Like a good many of his kind he's too over-confident, and he's given himself away on a number of counts. He made the very great mistake of committing murder, and as you know it's very hard to get away with that nowadays. What with Interpol the co-ordination between the various countries is amazingly good.'

I glanced up at my companion. She had dropped the mask and turned sickeningly pale. The hand which held the cigarette was trembling. She was staring straight ahead of her. I even began to feel a little sorry for her – till I remembered Steve.

'Yes, the police are just about ready to take Pierre whenever they want. All they're waiting for now is to find out who his associates are. Some of them may not realize that Pierre is wanted for murder, but they'll all have to face a charge of being accessories to murder. By the way, do they still use the guillotine here in Tunisia or has the Arab administration got its own method?'

The woman who called herself Audry Bryce threw down her cigarette.

In a very low voice and with a quite different intonation she said: 'I've had just about as much of this as I can take.'

Then she got up and walked away into the hotel.

I sat waiting for five, ten, fifteen minutes. At the end of that time a *chasseur* came on to the terrace.

'Paging Mr. Temple. Paging Mr. Temple.'

I lifted a finger and his sharp eyes picked me out at once. He came across to my table.

'You are wanted on the telephone, Mr. Temple.'

'Coming. Just hold on a minute.'

I tore a leaf from my pocket-book and scribbled on it.

'You might be glad of a friend on the police side. Could we not get together again?'

I folded it up and handed it to the *chasseur* with a thousand-franc note.

'Get that to the lady in room three seven one, but don't let anyone see you give it to her. If she's not alone make some excuse and wait till later.'

The *chasseur*, child though he was, winked naughtily at me and pocketed the money.

My telephone call was from Tony Wyse.

'Long time no see,' he said when he had announced himself. 'I'm sorry I haven't been round to visit you. I've been rather tied up with business and what not. Have you been savouring the delights of Tunis?'

'We've had a very eventful time so far.'

'That's good. Listen, I wondered if you and Mrs. Temple would dine with me this evening?'

'It's very kind of you, Wyse, but I'm afraid something has happened to my wife. She left the hotel early this morning and has not been seen since.'

'What?'

There was a stunned silence at the other end. Then Wyse said: 'Good God!' My news seemed to have hit him like a bombshell.

After a while he said: 'What have you done about it? Have you told the police?'

'Yes. I've told the police and they've tried all the hospitals. No luck.'

'This is terrible news. Look here, Temple, I've got to see you. Will you be there if I come over right away?'

I glanced at my watch. It would soon be time for me to leave if I was to keep my appointment with O'Halloran.

'No. I have to go out now. I have an appointment which I must keep.'

'Well, what about dining with me this evening in any case – even if you have to be on your own?'

'Well, I will if I can. Where shall we meet?'

'At the Hôtel Tunisie. It's at Sidi bou Saïd. A taxi will get you there in a quarter of an hour. Shall we say eight o'clock?'

'The Hôtel Tunisie at Sidi bou Saïd?'

'That's right. I'll be there at eight anyway, and you come as soon as you can.'

'I'll do my best.'

'Fine. See you then.'

I was smoking more than my normal quota of ciga-rettes. I lit another as I came out of the phone booth, and stood for a while watching the people walking through the hotel *foyer* or sitting waiting for a friend to appear. I kept checking in my mind, wondering whether there was some lead I had missed, some obvious step that I ought to be taking. There was no good in asking the desk yet again if there was any message for me. They could perfectly well see me where I was standing. Now it was six hours since I had last seen Steve, and there was still no message. Had something gone wrong? Had she put up too good a fight and been accidentally killed in the struggle? Then the worst thought of all hit me. Had she been taken not in order to blackmail me, but to find out how much we knew? Was someone spending all this time in trying to make her tell something she didn't even know?

For a moment a red film slimed across my eyes and I had to clench my fists. In spite of my resolution I was going towards the desk again, like a drug addict who must have another shot of dope. Perhaps a message had come in during the last few minutes.

The *chasseur* to whom I had given the note ran up and touched my elbow as I turned away, empty-handed, after another useless enquiry.

'I caught her just as she was getting into a taxi,' he said. 'No one saw me. She said to give you this.'

I nodded my thanks and opened the note. Underneath my own message these ten shaky words had been scribbled: 'Be in your room at midnight. I will come then.' The *chasseur* was still waiting in hopes. 'Get me a taxi,' I told him, and followed slowly as he darted towards the street.

Chapter Eight

KHÉRÉDINE is not far from Tunis straight across the lagoon as the crow flies, or as the railway runs. If you go by car you have to describe a half-circle, which takes you out to El Aouina airport on the road to Sidi bou Saïd. Khérédine is a curious quarter, part bathing beach, part luxury residential district, part dock area. My driver knew the Hotel du Port and took me unhesitatingly to a grimy street with houses on one side and an indeterminate waterfront on the other. This was the part where boat repairs were carried out, house-boats moored, and private motor-launches tied up. The Hôtel du Port was an old-fashioned café made more unappetizing by its yellowy strip lighting. I could see dockers in the bar at the front grouped round a billiard table. The strains of accordion music floated out through the open door.

When my taxi had driven away I felt that I was alone in a very foreign part of the world. The sun had gone down and been followed very swiftly by darkness. The moon was not yet up. The glow of Tunis seemed to be reflected down from the sky, and only beyond its halo did the stars seem bright. I could hear the small Mediterranean waves feeling their way in among the boats, slopping against the pylons of the wharf and gurgling up on to isolated little patches of sand.

I had omitted to ask O'Halloran on which side of the café Durant's house stood, but since the café was on a street corner the information was not necessary. The house was clearly used partly as residence and partly as offices. Durant's business sign had been painted across one of the ground-floor windows, and upstairs there were frilly lace curtains. I went up the steps and rang the bell, wondering whether this time I was really going to meet the elusive David Foster – and if not whom O'Halloran would produce to impersonate him.

The bell was answered by a slatternly woman with an apron tied round her middle and her sleeves rolled up to the elbow. Her hands were wet with soapy water and she had to push the hair out of her eyes with the back side of her wrist.

'The office is closed, *monsieur.*'

'I arranged to meet a Mr. O'Halloran here at seven o'clock. Has he arrived yet?'

'What name?'

'O'Halloran,' I said again, knowing full well that to French ears it must sound more Arabic than Irish.

She shook her head and pursed her lips.

'No one of that name here.'

'This is the house of *Monsieur* Durant?'

'Yes, this is *Monsieur* Durant's house.'

'Will you tell him that Mr. Temple is here? I think he is probably expecting me.'

'Tem-pel. Well he has gone out a little time ago. Is it urgent?'

'Yes,' I said. 'It is very urgent indeed.'

She shrugged her shoulders and sniffed resignedly.

'I will try and find him for you. You can wait here.'

She wiped her hands on a corner of her apron and opened the door of one of the ground floor rooms. She snapped on the light and left. I heard her close the front door and hurry down the steps. Durant's office was a litter of papers, files and blueprints. Dust lay thick on the shelves and floor. All the ash-trays were full to overflowing. The single bulb hanging from the middle of the ceiling shed a defeatist light over this scene of disorder. I realized that I must be fully visible to anyone outside, so I sat down in one of the chairs and lit one of my own cigarettes. I hoped that it might do something to dispel the odour of stale Gauloise smoke.

After ten minutes the conviction grew on me that I was being made a fool of and that O'Halloran had never had any intention of turning up. Here I was sitting inactive in a fly-blown office in Khérédine when at this very minute some message about Steve might be coming in to the hotel. I had been pretty sure at Zoltan Gupte's shop that neither he nor O'Halloran knew about her abduction. Why then was I wasting time out here?

I was about to pack the whole thing up when I heard footsteps in the street outside, and recognized the voice of the woman with the apron. She was with a man. They were squabbling violently.

Durant burst into the room, brimming over with apologies. He had been called over to the Port Office, he had explained, and had lost count of the time. He was one of those Frenchmen on whom the North African climate has a bad effect. He had run to flesh and the muscles of his face had gone slack. His colour was unnaturally high and I suspected that he drank too much. He looked about sixty, though he may not have been more than forty-seven.

'You were expecting me, then?'

'Yes, I had a message from *Monsieur* Zoltan Gupte, I hope you will overlook my being late, *monsieur*. I would not like *Monsieur* Zoltan Gupte to think that I had not done my best. Now if you will come with me down to the landing-stage I will take you out to the yacht.'

'The yacht? Is that where O'Halloran and Zoltan Gupte are?'

Durant was shepherding me out of the house. He seemed in a great hurry to make up for lost time.

'I do not know if *Monsieur* Zoltan Gupte is there, *monsieur*. I do not ask questions. I do as he tells me, that is all.'

'How long will it take to row out to the yacht?'

'Not long, *monsieur*. Maybe five minutes.'

Now that I was here I might as well carry through to the end.

I said: 'Make it as quick as you can. I haven't much time to spare.'

I found it rather remarkable that this Frenchman should adopt such a servile attitude towards a mere antique dealer from the Arab quarter. He was hurrying me through a maze of sheds and piles of timber at such a pace that I had no chance to ask him any questions. Presently our feet resounded on a small wooden jetty to which a number of rowing-boats were attached. Durant selected one of the smaller ones and put out a hand to steady me as I stepped aboard.

'This is not a work I usually do myself,' he explained, as he pushed off. 'But my employees have all gone home. Still, since it is for *Monsieur* Zoltan Gupte . . .'

'He is a man of considerable influence?' I observed.

'*Monsieur* Zoltan Gupte? You did not know that he is one of the richest men in Tunis? Some say he is a millionaire.'

'He has other irons in the fire besides his antique shop, then?'

'I do not enquire about that, *monsieur*. I ask no questions. He pays me well and that is enough.'

We were clear of the other boats now. After a glance over his shoulder Durant was heading at an oblique angle away from the shore. I could detect the dim outline of a large yacht moored some way out.

'Do you know a Mr. David Foster?'

'That is an English name, *monsieur*? No, I do not know of such a person.'

'Have you taken anyone else out to the yacht this evening?'

'No, *monsieur*. It is too early. Usually the gentlemen who visit the yacht come at ten, eleven – maybe midnight.'

'But you do know Mr. O'Halloran – he is a friend of Zoltan Gupte. A small Irishman with a couple of teeth missing.'

'Yes, I remember him, *monsieur*. Only four days ago I took him out to the yacht in this boat. Very sad. You saw about his death in the papers? These killings are becoming all too frequent in Tunis.'

The shore line had slid back into the darkness behind us. The surface of the sea was inky black and as smooth as if oil had been poured on it. The lights from the port installations sent reflexions wriggling across the water towards us. As we moved further out I could see the lights of the Arab quarter climbing the hill away behind Khérédine. Further to the right the gaunt heights of Hammam Lif rose like black-draped phantoms against an only slightly less dark sky. Curiously magnified sounds drifted out from the shore, seeming to slide across the water to us as easily as stones across a curling rink – the blaring radio from the Hôtel du Port, the honk of a car moving along the water-front, a sudden human cry, and behind it all the vague bustling ant-heap rumble of a big city. Somewhere not far off I could hear the rushing swish of a bow wave as a motor-boat moved fast towards the land.

After five minutes more of rowing the yacht loomed up ahead of us, her outlines clarifying with uncanny swiftness. She was carrying no lights and there was no sign of anyone on board.

Durant lifted his oars and hailed her as we drifted closer. There was no answer.

'I think we are too early,' he said. 'There is no one here yet. We'd better turn back.'

'There's a flight of steps on the port side. Pull alongside and I'll have a look on board.'

'Oh, I never go on board,' Durant said quickly.

'I'm not asking you to. But since we've come all this way don't you think I'd better make sure Zoltan Gupte is not waiting for me?'

Durant's expression was doubtful, but with the air of a man who does not accept any responsibility for what he is doing, he edged the boat close enough to the boarding steps for me to jump on to the yacht.

It was a fair-sized craft, about fifty feet long. Though it had originally been built to go to sea, it was obvious that recent alterations had turned it into more of an elaborate house-boat. The whole length of the deck had been built up, leaving only a narrow promenade round the outside.

I found a doorway which was unlocked. With the help of my pen torch I located the light switches and turned them all on. Most of the upper deck appeared to be taken up by a kind of club room. There was a bar at one end, a great many sofas and arm-chairs and a series of plush-covered snuggeries round the walls. The lighting was discreet and low. A few seconds after I had switched it on the radiogram emitted several mechanical clicks and then began to play a tango.

A proper staircase had been built to connect this room with the lower deck. Pressing switches down as I went I descended the steps. Ahead of me was a corridor with cabin doors opening to right and left. I began systematically to inspect them. Each one contained a comfortable couch, a dressing-table and mirror, wash-basin and *bidet*. Only the cabin at the far end of the corridor showed signs of permanent occupation. It was much larger than the others, and furnished as a bed-sitting-room. Several obvious signs showed that it was a man's, but that he was equipped to receive female visitors.

The smell of cigarette smoke was still quite fresh in the air and a faint perfume which reminded me of someone I had met recently.

A straight-backed chair had been placed in the middle of the room and several unfinished cigarette stubs lay on the carpet near it. One of the supports on the back of the chair had been broken. On the table lay a short length of stout cord which had been knotted and then cut with a knife. A man's dressing-gown had been thrown untidily on the bunk. The silk cord which should have been attached to it lay on the floor some distance away. I rolled it up and put it in my pocket.

A quick search of the cabin gave no indication of its occupant's identity, but under the lid of a complicated table which could be used as a desk I found a detailed plan of Tunis. Someone had drawn a circle round the Hôtel François Premier, and a red line showed the route which Steve and I had followed on each of our outings. Also encircled in red were the House of Shoni, a street corner in the Rue de Rome, and several other points which meant nothing to me.

I folded it up and put it in my pocket.

The brutal scene which had taken place so recently in the cabin had left its unsavoury impression on the atmosphere as clearly as a picture stamps itself on the negative of a film. I had a feeling that time was running short. Snapping the lights off as I went I regained the deck and climbed quickly down into Durant's boat.

Durant seemed glad to get away from the yacht, and pushed off with enthusiasm.

'What time was it when Zoltan Gupte gave you your instructions?' I asked him.

'About two o'clock this afternoon.'

'Don't you think it rather odd that he should have made these elaborate arrangements and then failed to turn up?'

'I don't know,' Durant said, putting his full weight on to the oars. 'All I know is I was told to bring a *Monsieur* Tem-pel out to the yacht at seven this evening.'

The oar struck something in the water which threw Durant out of his rhythm. He pulled his oar in to clear he obstacle. The boat glided on under its own impetus and he swung forward to make the next stroke.

'Hold on a second,' I said. 'Did you see what that was in the water?'

'No.'

'I think it was a body. A woman's body.'

Time went into low gear, while Durant manœuvred his boat round. Every detail of the scene stamped itself on my mind. I had only caught a glimpse of the dark shape in the water, but I had been left with no doubt that it was a human form.

'There it is over there,' Durant called, and began to row with one oar and backpedal with the other.

A dark bundle, which seemed to be part of the sea itself, was breaking the surface and then sinking just below it again.

I leaned over the side towards it. I could see a head and long hair drifting out from it.

'Look out or you'll capsize the boat!' Durant shouted. 'Just keep still till I can get nearer.'

He had probably found bodies in the water before, and had no idea what I was going through. He edged the boat a little closer, then shipped his oars and made a grab over the side.

'I have a hold of it. Goodness knows how long it's been in the water. You haven't a torch, have you?'

Durant had been struggling to lift the head of the drowned person. My stomach was coming up into my mouth, but I forced myself to direct my torch down towards the water.

The boat gave a great rock. Durant gasped: 'I can't do it.'

He relinquished his hold and the form slipped down into the black waters again. Just for a moment a darkened face was turned up towards my torch beam and I recognized the features of Audry Bryce.

Less time had elapsed than I had imagined, and it was only ten past eight when once again I entered the Hôtel François Premier. Although it was now inevitable that I would be very late for my appointment with Tony Wyse, I was determined to check in there before doing anything else.

By the time Durant had rowed me back to the landing-stage I had recovered from the dreadful shock of finding the body in the water, and managed to prevent him from seeing that I had recognized Audry Bryce. He had undertaken to inform the police and agreed to leave me out of his report. I had come back from Khérédine on one of the frequent trains, and found that just as quick as using a taxi.

'Mrs. Temple has not returned,' the receptionist informed me, anticipating my question before I had time to ask it. 'She has been gone a long time, *monsieur*. Have you thought of notifying the police?'

'I've done that already. They're doing all they can. Listen, I shall be dining at the Hôtel Tunisie in Sidi bou Saïd. Will you make yourself personally responsible for telephoning me there if there is any news?'

'I will do that with pleasure, *monsieur*.'

This receptionist was more *sympathique* than his predecessor, and his manner showed genuine concern.

I had noticed one of the assistant clerks answering the telephone at the back of the office. She came now to the desk.

'Someone from Police Headquarters to speak to *Monsieur* Temple.'

'Put it through to box number one,' the receptionist said. 'You can take it in the first box, Mr. Temple.'

My hopes had soared unreasonably during the few seconds that it took me to reach the telephone booth. I pushed the door shut and put the instrument to my ear.

'Temple speaking.'

'*Allo*. It is *Monsieur* Temple who is speaking? One moment, please.'

I waited impatiently, knocking with my knuckles on the glass partition.

'Hallo, Temple. That you?'

There was no mistaking the voice which I had heard addressing me so frequently across a desk in Scotland Yard.

'Sir Graham! Thank God you've arrived.'

'Just got in about half an hour ago. I'm at the *Commissariat de Police* with Renouk. Temple, I'm very sorry to hear this news about Steve.'

'It's not too good, is it?'

'No. But the police are really on the war path. It's only a question of time till they find her.'

'I hope you're right, Sir Graham. But I confess I'm worried. Any chance of you coming over here right away?'

'Afraid not. I have some very urgent business here first. But I want to see you later this evening. Will you be there if I come along at eleven?'

'Yes, I'll be here. And, by the way, Sir Graham . . .'

'Yes?'

'How do you come to turn up in Tunis at this particular moment?'

I heard Forbes chuckle.

'Shall we just say that I'm here on account of a very special pair of spectacles?'

Before I could question him he had rung off.

It was significant of my change of attitude that I did not take Renouk the map which I had found on board the yacht. Instead, I asked the receptionist for an envelope, sealed the map inside it, and asked him to put it in his cash safe so that I could pick it up whenever I wanted.

If I had had to submit my expense account for that day to an auditor, he would undoubtedly have made objections to the vast sums I was spending on taxis. I chartered yet another one for the trip out to Sidi bou Saïd.

Wyse, I reflected, as I was borne rapidly northwards, was about the last string to my bow. For some reason Zoltan Gupte and O'Halloran had been scared off meeting me as arranged. I had a feeling that even if I went to the House of Shoni I would find it locked and shuttered. Perhaps the idea had occurred to Renouk that Steve's disappearance was a sequel to our meeting with him, and the attentions of the police had decided the pair to lie low. If only

I could have followed up my conversation with Audry Bryce more swiftly. Her promise to come to my room at midnight might have been the bait for a trap, but I was more inclined to believe that I really had thrown her into a scare, and that she had decided to take my advice and line herself up with the right side. Someone had sensed that she was cracking and had made sure that she could tell no tales out of school.

The Hôtel Tunisie occupied a beautiful site on a high promontory which jutted out into the sea. Beyond the buildings the ground fell away steeply to a beach far below, and a terrace had been built out from which guests could command a magnificent view along the coast past Carthage to Tunis itself. Beyond that the eye followed the curve of the land right round to the Cap Bon peninsula.

A corridor led past the dining-room entrance towards the floodlit terrace, on which I could already see a number of people sitting round their *apéritifs*. My way through was momentarily barred by a fair-haired man who was talking to the head waiter. The latter was showing him the greatest deference.

'*Maitre d'hôtel,*' I heard the fair-haired man say in French. 'You will have a table for two for me? I am dining with an American friend this evening. Do you know if a Mr. Vandenberg has arrived yet?'

'*Mais oui, monsieur,*' the head waiter gesticulated towards the terrace with the evening's menu card. 'Mr. Vandenberg is already arrived. He awaits you on the terrace.'

'Good. I will join him as soon as I have given my orders to the wine waiter.'

I waited for Schultz to move on out of my way. He had been quite unaware that I had been standing at his elbow.

'Has Mr. Wyse come yet?' I asked the head waiter.

'Is it Mr. Temple? Mr. Wyse asked me to tell you that he is in the terrace bar. Outside and to your left, *monsieur.*'

I made a mental note that when this was over and Steve and I were together again, we would come and spend some time at the Hôtel Tunisie. It was an almost perfect setting. The terrace seemed to be poised in the velvet darkness, a little oasis of luxury created by the genius of man working in perfect harmony with what nature had supplied. Just at this moment my mind could not take in its beauty. I was too preoccupied with grim realities.

I was crossing the terrace towards the bar built at the end when my attention was attracted by a solitary figure sitting at one of the tables. His eyes had been on the doorway when I emerged, and he had looked away with peculiar abruptness. As I passed him I noticed how his ears were set and the distinctive shape of the back of his head. The disguise was good, but those two features were familiar. He had long, wispy, grey hair and the lined, sallow complexion of the American business man who is suffering from ulcers. He wore octagonal spectacles. A light-grey, broad-brimmed hat lay on the table. His suit was of obviously American cut.

I checked in my stride and laid a hand on the back of his chair.

'Good evening, Colonel Rostand. How nice to see you again!'

The old gentleman turned his sad, worry-ridden expression towards me, and eyed me with tolerant disapproval. It was very well done.

'I'm afraid you're making a mistake, young man. My name is Vandenberg. Henry O. Vandenberg.'

The accent was American, and the intonation not unlike that of the unseen Pierre whom I had overheard in conclave

155

with Audry Bryce. I was amused to note that he lisped his *s*'s. A tongue split by a blow on the chin could account for that.

'I'm so sorry, sir,' I apologized. 'It was a silly mistake. It's just that I have something which I very badly wanted to return to this Colonel Rostand.'

'Oh?'

There was a flicker of interest behind the glinting spectacles.

'Yes, I'm sure he'll be very distressed when he finds he hasn't got it.'

'Say, that's too bad. What was this you found?'

Rostand had been unable to suppress his curiosity. I put my hand in my pocket and brought out the rolled up silk dressing-gown cord.

'This piece of cord was used to strangle a woman on a yacht lying off Khérédine this evening. Her name was Audry Bryce. After she had been murdered her body was thrown into the sea.'

Perhaps I should not have said anything, just shown him the cord. He appeared to shrink a little when I first produced it, but my short speech gave him time to recover. He pushed his chair back and stood up.

'Young man,' he declared, 'I don't know who you are, but if this is your idea of a wisecrack then you've chosen the wrong man to pull it on.'

He turned his back on me and marched towards the hotel entrance. Though he affected a slight stoop he was unable to mask his considerable height. I was still standing with the cord in my hand when Schultz emerged from the separate door which led to the dining-room from the terrace.

He saw me at once and his eyes narrowed. Yet by the time he reached me he was smiling.

'Good evening, Mr. Temple.' There still seemed to be that ironic undercurrent in his words. 'Your charming wife is not with you?'

'Not this evening,' I said shortly. 'I'm surprised that you're not at Le Trou du Diable.'

'I was invited to dinner, Mr. Temple. That happens even to us *restaurateurs*, you know.'

'By the rich American, Mr. Vandenberg?'

'That is so. How did you know?'

'Should we not give him his real name and call him Colonel Rostand?'

Schultz assumed a bewildered expression and spread out his hands appealingly.

'Always this talk of Colonel Rostand, Mr. Temple. I think you have some complex about him. I assure you Mr. Vandenberg is very well known here.'

'I'm glad of that for your sake, Mr. Schultz. Colonel Rostand is still being sought by the police.'

'By the way' – Schultz took a gold cigarette-case from his breast pocket, offered me one, and then lit his own – 'talking of the police. Inspector Flambeau told me an extraordinary thing: that you had been asked to deliver a pair of spectacles to a man named David Foster, and that *Monsieur* Constantin had offered you ten thousand pounds for them. Is that story true?'

'It is quite true.'

'But have you any idea,' Schultz persisted, 'why a pair of spectacles should have such a disproportionate value and attract the interest of so many people?'

'I have an idea. And as so many people are interested, Mr. Schultz, I wondered if you could be one of them?'

Schultz shook his head and the corners of his mouth twitched in a smile.

'Why should I be interested, Mr. Temple? My eyesight is perfect. Now, if you will excuse me, I must find my guest.'

When he had gone I continued my progress towards the bar, and found Wyse staring moodily at the bubbles in his champagne cocktail, as if he'd abandoned all hope of my ever appearing. He brightened up when he saw me, but showed concern on noting that I had come alone.

'Still no news of your wife? This is terrible, terrible.'

He was so genuinely distressed that my heart warmed to him.

'Why should anyone want to harm Mrs. Temple?'

I decided at that moment to take a chance and let Wyse into my confidence. I was getting nowhere with the kind of shadow boxing I had indulged in with Rostand and Schultz.

'Let's find a table where we can talk,' I suggested. 'I'll tell you all about it.'

'I've booked a table for dinner. We can go in straight away if you like.'

I was not really interested in food, but Wyse insisted on my ordering a decent meal, which was certainly a good thing in the end. I was going to need every calorie before that long night ended.

While we ate I told him almost the whole story: how we had met Judy Wincott in Paris, my promise to deliver the spectacles, the series of murders which had dogged us in Nice, Algiers and now Tunis. He listened with concentrated attention, only interrupting me with an occasional brief question. He seemed a good deal less the empty-headed playboy than before.

'It's a most extraordinary story,' he said when I had finished. 'Obviously you've run into something very big indeed. But how on earth can a pair of spectacles have enough value to justify five murders?'

'I would be very glad if you could tell me.'

'By the sound of it there are several separate gangs. I mean, Rostand and Schultz must be hand in glove with Leyland and the late lamented Audry Bryce. Constantin seems to have been a lone wolf – unless he was connected with Zoltan Gupte and O'Halloran. The important thing from your point of view is to know which group have kidnapped Steve – I mean Mrs. Temple.'

'You've left one person out.'

'Oh? Who's that?'

'Simone Lalange. She has a way of turning up every now and again which cannot be accidental. Where do you fit her in?'

'Simone?' Wyse was looking very youthful and worried. 'You don't seriously believe she's involved in all this?'

'I forgot to tell you that on the evening when we discovered Judy Wincott's body in that room, Steve picked up an empty book of matches outside the door. It was the replica of the ones Simone carries.'

'Oh, that's easy,' Wyse exclaimed with relief. 'She told me herself that she'd turned the room down because it hadn't a bathroom. She must have dropped the book of matches when she was being shown the room.'

'None the less,' I said, 'I'm sure there's more to Mademoiselle Lalange than meets the eye.'

'No, you're quite off the rails there, Temple.'

He stubbed his cigarette out a little too forcibly in his coffee saucer.

'I wish I could help you. There's nothing more that you haven't told me? I'm very sorry you have not brought those spectacles with you. I'd give anything to have a look at them.'

'Would you? What about lunching with my wife and me at the François Premier to-morrow? I'll show them to you then. We could invite Simone Lalange too.'

159

'That's rather a good idea . . .' Wyse began enthusiastically. Then he stopped. 'But you said with your wife and you. Supposing Mrs. Temple—'

'Supposing I have not found her by then? In that case I will not be able to show you the spectacles. If the people have made no proposal by to-morrow morning I'm going to smash those glasses to smithereens. Now, if you don't mind, I must be getting back to the hotel.'

'I have a car outside,' Wyse said, rousing himself out of his reverie and signalling to the waiter. 'I'll run you into Tunis.'

I could probably have picked Wyse's car out from among those standing in the park even if he had not been there to guide me. It was a two-seater M.G., of a rather hideous green colour. He unzipped the tonneau cover which protected the two small seats.

'You don't mind a bit of air? I can put the hood up if you like.'

'I shall be all right,' I said, and inserted my legs into the narrow tunnel provided for them.

The gravel of the car park was sent flying as we accelerated out on to the road. The rear tyres screamed as soon as they were on the tarmac. Wyse caned his engine mercilessly, and the car jerked at each successive gear change. The noise of the wind made conversation impossible. I grasped the alarming handle fixed to the dashboard and tried to appreciate the beauties of the landscape.

We swept down the hill from Sidi bou Saïd, leaving behind us the luxurious villas of the rich Arab merchants of Tunis. Soon we were screaming past Carthage, the headlights sending long warning beams down the road ahead of us.

Wyse seemed anxious to show me his car's cornering powers, and as we rushed towards a fast left-hand bend he pulled well over to the wrong side of the road so as to cut the corner. I grasped the chromium-plated handle more firmly and tried to assume an Arabic attitude of fatalism.

Wyse spun the steering-wheel, and I felt as if my elbow was about to break through the side of the car. The tail began to slide outwards. Wyse rapidly put on the opposite lock in an attempt to correct the skid. But his move had no effect on the behaviour of the car. I saw him juggling madly with a steering-wheel which had suddenly gone slack. The car was gyrating wildly, and all the time its impetus was carrying us towards the ditch and bank that bordered the road. The tail was pointing backwards as we hit the grass verge with a bump that nearly shook us out of our seats. The car had time to spin through a hundred and eighty degrees before we slammed into the bank. I saw the bonnet go up in the air and instinctively crouched down in my seat. For an agonizing instant the car stood on its tail, then with apparent slowness it toppled back on top of us.

It was the ditch which prevented us from being crushed underneath it. The car lay straddling the slight dip, depositing Wyse and me on our heads in a dried-up water course. Close to me I could hear the trickle of petrol escaping from the filler cap. The car could catch fire at any moment. There was just room to crawl out under the door beside me. I squeezed through and stood up, to find Wyse standing on the other side.

'Phew! That was a near one!'

He stared back at the skid marks corkscrewing across the road towards us.

'I wasn't going too fast, you know. I could have corrected that skid easily, only the steering went dead on me.'

He seemed more concerned about disclaiming responsibility for the accident than about the fact that he had only just failed to kill us both. I suppose the passenger, who can do nothing except watch helplessly, always has the worse time on these occasions.

I went far enough away from the wrecked car to strike a light in safety. I put a cigarette in my mouth and lit it. Wyse had managed to reach into his glove compartment and find a torch. I saw him examining the front axle of the M.G. After several minutes he came towards me, looking very thoughtful.

'Somebody is not very kindly disposed towards yours truly. That was a piece of deliberate sabotage.'

'How do you mean?'

'The drag link had been forced out of its socket and was only held by a piece of wire. It was bound to snap as soon as any strain was put on it.'

We were lucky to stop an empty cab returning from Sidi bou Saïd. Wyse dropped me at my hotel before going on to a garage to arrange for the salvage of his car.

'Don't forget,' he called through the window just before the taxi drove off. 'We have a date for lunch to-morrow. You haven't forgotten your promise?'

I said: 'I always keep my promises.'

Chapter Nine

SIR GRAHAM FORBES had been waiting for a bare five minutes when I found him in the writing-room of the hotel, his spectacles perched on his nose and a typewritten memorandum on his knee.

'Sorry to keep you waiting, Sir Graham. I had a little accident on the way.'

'It's good to see you, Temple.' Sir Graham came to meet me with outstretched hand.

We were both struck with a momentary awkwardness. Sir Graham and I had met in a good many strange places, but there had nearly always been another person there, and we had abruptly become painfully conscious of Steve's absence.

'I'm glad you've come,' I said. 'I am very much in need of a friend.'

'I understand. Where can we go to talk without being disturbed?'

'My room's the best place, I think.'

The hotel *foyer* was almost deserted as we crossed it towards the lift. The François Premier was an extremely respectable hotel, which calmed down early every evening.

'By the way,' Sir Graham said as the lift bore us upwards, 'I promised the receptionist to give you a message. Some chap has been telephoning you every quarter of an hour since ten o'clock. Name of Leyland.'

'Leyland? What did he want?'

'Wouldn't say, apparently. Just kept asking if Mr. Temple was in.'

'Do they know where he was calling from?'

'I don't think so. The chap wouldn't say much.'

'Well, if he rings again they'll put the call through to my room.'

As we walked along the corridor to room number three seven one I noticed that the door of Audry Bryce's room was open and a chamber-maid was making the bed. I put my head in through the door and asked her when the room had been vacated.

'During dinner-time, sir. The lady's staying with friends. The chauffeur came to fetch her baggage.'

'Very thorough,' I said as I rejoined Forbes and inserted the key in my own lock.

'What's that?'

'Nothing. I'll explain later.'

I closed the door and bolted it. Then wound up the sunshade to let some air into the room, which was still close after the heat of the day. Forbes sat down in one of the easy-chairs while I picked up the receiver to call the reception desk.

'If any calls come in put them through to this room, will you? And you remember that envelope I asked you to look after for me? Would you send a page up with it right away?'

I turned back to Sir Graham, who had unrolled his tobacco pouch on to his knee and was filling his pipe.

'Now, Sir Graham. Let's have the answer to this mystery. It's not true that your doctor ordered you a complete rest?'

'I'm afraid that was all a story, Temple. I didn't want too much talk about what I was doing. The fact is I've been in Paris for the last few months, working in liaison with Interpol.'

'You told me on the telephone that you came here on account of a pair of spectacles. Do you mind elaborating on that remark?'

Forbes puffed at his pipe for a few moments and the flame of the match bobbed up and down over the bowl.

'I'm relying on you to do some elaborating for me, Temple. But would I be right in saying that when you were in Paris you acquired a pair of spectacles which have involved you in a certain amount of embarrassment?'

'Embarrassment? That deserves a prize for understatement! Several people have been murdered, almost under our very noses; I've been threatened with shooting, escaped miraculously from a car crash, whilst my wife has been kidnapped. And you call that embarrassing?'

Forbes had created a grey cloud in the atmosphere above his head, and was thickening it up with every breath.

'Come to that,' I said. 'How do you know about all this?'

'Interpol's a wonderful organization. We've been following your adventures ever since you were interviewed by Mirabel in Nice. A smart man, that.'

He broke off as a knock sounded on the door. I went to unbolt it and handed a tip to the page who had brought up the envelope. Sir Graham raised his eyebrows enquiringly, but when he saw that I was waiting to hear what he had to say he cleared his throat and went on.

'Your unfortunate experiences happen to tie up with a case on which I have been working with Interpol. You've heard of the Melrose jewels?'

'Who hasn't? One of the most valuable private collections in Britain. They were stolen from the Duke of Melrose's castle at the end of last year. The news of the robbery caused a sensation. Didn't the thieves tunnel under the castle walls from a cottage just outside and come up directly beneath the family treasure vault?'

'Yes. A most daring and well-conceived robbery. It wasn't discovered until four days later, and the thieves got away with stuff to the value of close on half a million.'

'And this is the case you've been working on?'

Forbes, as usual, had packed his tobacco too tight. It had gone out, and he had to apply another match and hold his box over the bowl to make it draw.

'The robbery was planned by a syndicate, but the brains and uniting force behind the whole thing was a chap called Leather.'

'Leather?'

'Yes. Adrian Leather, an international criminal. You know the name?'

'Yes, I know it. Sorry to interrupt. Go on.'

'Well, they managed to get the stuff out of Britain, and we still don't know how. But we do know that they got as far as Tunisia before the hunt came too close to them. Leather hid the jewels, making a careful note of the hiding-place, and the syndicate agreed to split up and wait till things were quieter before they started to sell the stuff. However—'

Forbes took his pipe out of his mouth and thoughtfully contemplated the dead ash in the bowl.

'—all the best laid schemes of mice and so on. Three months later Leather was crossing a street in Paris when he was hit by a car and received multiple injuries. He survived for a few days in hospital before dying. During that time a woman who was devoted to him never left his side—'

'Mrs. Audry Leather,' I said confidently.

'No,' Forbes contradicted. 'You're quite wrong. This girl was called Diana Simmonds.'

'Diana Simmonds! By Timothy! That's the name of the girl who was found murdered outside our flat in Paris!'

'Correct. Now the interesting thing—'

Forbes broke off. The telephone was ringing. I stood up and crossed the room to it.

'Hullo. Temple speaking.'

'This is reception, *monsieur*. A Mr. Leyland is here to see you.'

'He's here – in the hotel?'

'Yes, *monsieur*.'

'You'd better tell him to come up.'

'Very good, *monsieur*.'

During the time that I estimated it would take Leyland to come up in the lift I gave Sir Graham an idea of where he fitted into the picture. I was unlocking the door when I heard the familiar rumble of the lift doors opening. Perhaps ten seconds later Forbes and I both recognized a sound which once heard can never be forgotten – the thwack of a silenced automatic. It took perhaps two seconds for the implications to hit us, another three for me to unlock the door and wrench it open.

In the corridor the burly form of Sam Leyland lay twitching on the ground. His hands were both clamped to his back and he was arching his spine in pain. Beyond him the lift doors were closing – just too quickly for me to see whoever was inside.

'Telephone the hall,' I called back to Sir Graham. 'Tell them to stop whoever comes out of the lift.'

I ran towards Sam Leyland and dropped on one knee beside him. He struggled to rise to his knees.

'Take it easy,' I said. 'Don't move more than you need.'

'Don't worry about me. Get that bastard,' he grunted.

Sir Graham and I bumped in the doorway of the bedroom.

'I've told them,' he said. 'They're watching the lift.'

Over his shoulder I could see the receiver, still off its cradle, lying on its side on the table.

'Help me to get him in and on to the bed.'

Together we lifted Leyland into the room and laid him on the bed. While Forbes went back to the telephone I split Leyland's jacket up the back and ripped his shirt open. The bullet had gone in through a neat hole just below his ribs. It probably had not improved one of his kidneys, but it had missed the heart. The bullet was still inside him.

'They've got another think coming if they're counting on that stopping Sam Leyland,' growled my patient. 'That swine shot me in the back.'

'Did you see who it was?'

'No. But it was one of Rostand's lot. Ooh, how I'd love three minutes in the ring alone with Rostand! Ouch!'

Leyland had tried to twist round, but as quickly decided to stay put. Forbes had replaced the telephone.

'The lift never came down,' he said. 'Our man must have got out at the first or second floor. He's probably gone out via the fire escape or the tradesmen's entrance by now. I told them to send for an ambulance, and the police. How's the patient?'

'Not so bad,' Sam Leyland said, though he was gasping with pain. 'I may have gone down for a count, but I still have my eyes open. You know it's a funny thing, I don't seem to feel much pain. A bit as if a rather feeble horse had kicked me in the back. Just danged cold.'

'It's shock. You'll feel that bullet all right when it wears off.'

'Temple—'

'Yes?'

'I came here to tell you something. I'm danged well going to say it. If you want to see your wife again let Rostand have those spectacles.'

'Have you seen Steve? Do you know where she is?'

In my eagerness I had gripped his arm more fiercely than I realized.

'No, chum. I can't tell you where they've got her, but I do know that she's still alive. And that's more than you can say for that poor Bryce girl. That's what decided me to quit. Murder's not in my line of business.'

'What's your line of business, Leyland?'

'Well, I've done a lot of things in my time, you know. But this offer Rostand made me was the best I've had. Four thousand quid for pinching a pair of spectacles. It was money for old rope.'

'Do you know why Rostand wanted the spectacles?'

'Not me, chum. I don't believe in asking too many questions. I say, would it do me any harm to smoke a fag?'

With my help he eased himself carefully on to his back and let me light the cigarette for him.

'Did you enjoy your little bit of motor-boating at Nice?' I enquired casually. 'That came pretty close to murder, didn't it?'

'That was Rostand's idea, not mine,' Leyland said sullenly. 'He thought you'd handed the glasses over to the police for good, and decided you'd be better out of the way.'

'So Rostand was in Nice too? Tell me, Sam, what really happened at the Villa Negra? Why was Thompson beaten up and shot?'

Leyland pulled deeply on his cigarette. I could see that his wound was beginning to hurt him. His face was a nasty grey

169

colour and his voice kept checking. I hoped the ambulance
men would come quickly.

'I won't say he deserved what he got, but he was too
greedy. A hundred quid for telling you he was David
Foster! Then after he'd phoned you at the Hotel Alletti
he thought he could put his price up. Rostand didn't quite
see it his way.'

Forbes had been on the balcony looking down into the
street. I knew by the way he came into the room that the
ambulance had arrived.

'One more thing, Sam. Am I right in thinking that Rostand
and Schultz are working together?'

'They are now. They joined forces in Algiers after you
came to the Villa Negra.'

'Did you ever see anything of Constantin or O'Halloran
and a man named Zoltan Gupte?'

Sam Leyland furrowed his brow and made an effort to
remember. He gave a sudden wince of pain.

'By God, that were like a red-hot knife in my back! No.
I never saw any of them. By the way Rostand talked about
them they belonged to another gang.'

Outside in the corridor could be heard the sound of voices
and a great clattering as something bulky was brought out
of the lift. Sam Leyland put a hand on my arm.

'You'll say a good word to the police for Sam Leyland,
Mr. Temple? I've done what I can to help you.'

The next moment Renouk burst into the room with
the posse. The ambulance men took Leyland away quite
promptly, but we could not get rid of Renouk till we had
made full statements about the shooting. I gave him a résumé
of as much of the information Leyland had given us as I
thought would be useful to him.

170

It was with relief that Forbes and I saw the door close on the last of the policemen.

'Things are beginning to move,' Forbes said. 'I think Renouk will soon put the cat among the pigeons.'

'But we're still no nearer our main objective, Sir Graham.'

'Steve? No, you're right there. But they're bound to make some move soon. They're bound to. And when they do we've got to have our plans cut and dried. What you have to decide, Temple, is whether you're going to agree to hand those spectacles over in exchange for the safe return of your wife.'

'I'm not in a position to do so, Sir Graham. Not before ten o'clock to-morrow morning. They're locked away in the vaults of Lloyds Bank.'

Forbes permitted himself the rare vulgarity of emitting a low whistle.

'This puts a very different complexion on things. What made you decide to do that?'

'It's a long story,' I warned him.

'I think I'd better hear it.'

I gave Forbes a full account of everything that had occurred since the moment when I had first set eyes on Judy Wincott at Fouquet's in Paris. He listened without a single interruption, making occasional jottings in his pocket-book. When I had finished he went through the list of questions he had noted to clear up the points about which he had been in doubt.

'I think that's pretty clear. And I agree with your appreciation of what Rostand's next move will be under the present circumstances. Now, I have my own ideas, Temple, but in view of the fact that Steve is in pawn, as it were, I feel it's up to you to suggest what should be done.'

'Right,' I said, and spread out the map of Tunis which I had found on board the yacht. 'Here's what I suggest. My

171

guess is that the circles marked on this map indicate the various buildings in which the gang have an interest. For instance, the House of Shoni and this hotel are so marked. Crosses indicate where certain incidents were to happen. I believe that cross on the Rue de Rome indicates where Steve was kidnapped, for instance.'

'I follow you. Would it not be advisable to ask the police to raid all these places without delay?'

'With Steve inside? Do you place such faith in the Tunisian Police Force?'

Forbes acknowledged my point with a wry, sideways inclination of the head.

'No,' I went on. 'My first object is to get to where Steve is and be with her when the balloon goes up. Now, if you were in Rostand's place what would you do?'

Forbes sniffed twice and rubbed his chin. He felt in his pocket, and I knew that I would have to watch him go through all that business with his pipe again.

'Well,' he said after a moment's thought. 'After encountering you at the Hôtel Tunisie and knowing that the police were turning Tunis upside down, I would decide that something had to be done without delay. If I have been playing on your nerves, I would consider that by now you were in quite a flap. I would wait till the small hours of the morning, when a man's morale is at its lowest, and then I would put the pressure on you.'

'How would you do that? By telephone?'

'Yes. But I'd know that any incoming calls to you could be traced by the police. I'd ring you from a call-box, and tell you that if you wanted to see your wife alive you'd better present yourself pronto with the spectacles at a point to be named by me.'

'That's what I think too. And when that call comes through I shall undoubtedly have to move very quickly. It will rest with you to organize the counter-attack. When you've had the call traced you can plot the position of the call-box on that map and decide which of the marked houses to put your money on. But I rely on you to stop Renouk from staging an artillery duel—'

'You're taking a big chance,' Forbes said thoughtfully. 'And there's another thing. Isn't Mr. Rostand going to cut up pretty rough when he finds you've gone empty-handed?'

I didn't answer for a moment, but looked at Sir Graham speculatively.

'What are you looking at me like that for?'

'Sir Graham—'

'Yes?'

'Would it be terribly inconvenient for you to part with your spectacles for a time?'

He was still gazing at me in astonishment when the telephone rang. We both glanced towards it quickly and our eyes met. I walked to the bedside table on which the instrument stood. There had been so many calls during the day that I tried to tell myself that this was not the vital one. But even as I lifted the receiver I felt it somehow alive in my hand.

'Temple speaking.'

'Listen, Temple. You want to see your wife again – alive?'

'Yes.'

'Then listen carefully and obey these instructions quickly and accurately.' The voice was muffled and harsh as if its owner were speaking behind a handkerchief and straining to disguise his pronunciation. 'You are being watched all the time. If you try to trick us or to contact the police your wife will be dying when you get to her. You understand me?'

173

Francis Durbridge

'Yes. Get on with it.'

'You have the spectacles with you?'

'Yes.'

'I hope you are telling the truth. Within ten seconds of my ringing off you will leave your room, and within half a minute you will emerge from the hotel. A cab will be waiting just opposite the hotel on the far side of the street. You will get into it. You heard that?'

'*Yes.*'

'Then you have forty seconds from now.'

There was a click and the line was dead. I glanced at the long hand on my watch which marked the seconds.

'I didn't recognize the voice,' I told Sir Graham. 'I have to move fast. Will you lend me your glasses?'

Forbes, with a slightly sad look, handed me his spectacles. They were remarkably similar to the pair reposing in Lloyds Bank, with strong broad ear-pieces. I tucked them into my outside breast pocket and replaced the handkerchief over them.

'The rest is up to you,' I told him. 'Good luck.'

'Good luck to you, Temple,' he said quietly, his hand on my shoulder.

I was walking down the corridor twelve seconds after the call had ended. That meant I had to make up two seconds on my trip to the hotel entrance. I had no doubt that my unseen caller had meant everything he said. Rostand was thorough enough to have even worked out the minimum time I would need to get down.

The indicator lights outside the lift showed me that it was on the ground floor. I would have to use the stairs. I leapt down them four at a time. Between the second and first floor I met a waiter carrying a tray of drinks up to someone's

174

room. I hit him square amidships. He crumpled back against the wall and the glasses went flying.

As I careered on I heard him hurling most unwaiterly comments after me.

I had eight seconds in hand when my feet touched the ground floor. The *foyer* was deserted now, but as the Hotel François Premier offered a twenty-four hour service, there was still a clerk at the reception desk. He gaped when he saw me sprint across the brilliant carpet that had once graced a Royal Palace in Egypt. I slowed to a walk as I came to the hotel doors. The side glass panels had been closed, and I had to push my way through a swing door.

Behind me I heard the night receptionist call out: 'Mr. Temple! Oh, Mr. Temple!' but I had no time for him.

I stood for a moment under the canopy which extended over the section of pavement outside the hotel. I was dead on time. The streets were not quite deserted, and many of the café lights were still burning. There were a surprising number of pedestrians about. Tunis was not so dead as London would have been at this hour of the night. There were still cabs in the rank along the street, but opposite me I could see a solitary taxi drawn up at the kerb. The white blob of the driver's face was turned in my direction. As I walked across the road towards him he reached out a hand and opened the door of the rear compartment.

No word was said as I climbed in and shut the door. He already had his engine running. All he had to do was engage the gear and drive off. I was surprised that I was being allowed such comfort and freedom. I could see exactly where we were going and make a note of the route.

The driver took me northwards and through a maze of streets that eventually emerged on a long, tree-lined boulevard running all along the east side of the modern quarter of Tunis. It was deserted at this hour. After some distance my driver pulled towards the kerb and stopped.

'Here you will get out,' he said. 'Continue to walk in this direction. Keep close to the edge of the kerb. Do not stop or speak to anyone.'

'How much do I owe you?' I asked him as I got out. He did not take the joke. Instead he uttered the five-letter French word.

I started along the apparently interminable boulevard. Behind me the taxi-driver had doused his lights. The palm trees planted at regular intervals along the boulevard were etched clearly against a night sky brilliant with an unbelievable multitude of stars.

I had gone a quarter of a mile when I noticed that the bole of the palm tree which I was passing was illuminated by the lights of a car coming up behind me. I saw my own shadow lengthen in the yellowy light of the cadmium bulbs. The car swished past within inches of me. It was a large American model the size of a cruiser. It stopped a few yards past me and the rear door opened.

'Get in,' a voice invited me.

I stooped to enter, and immediately put my head into a thick bag of some coarse material. A pair of hands pulled me forward and downwards, and another pair yanked me on to the floor of the car. I heard the door slam.

'Make no trouble,' a dangerous voice commanded me in French. 'Just keep still where you are.'

I made myself reasonably comfortable and obeyed my instructions. I could feel the car gathering speed. It was a good thing that I had not tried to have myself followed. Rostand's methods of abduction had made sure that any shadower would have been detected. I supposed that ten minutes must have passed since the call came through. I wondered how much luck Forbes would have in tracing it.

With the sack over my head I could not tell how long the journey lasted. We seemed to be turning a great many corners, and I guessed that the driver was making sure he was not being followed. After that our speed seemed to mount and I heard the whine of the tyres on the tarmac of a main road. The sound continued for a long time and my heart sank as I realized I was being taken some way out of Tunis. We must already be beyond the confines of the map I had left with Forbes.

Presently the car slowed and there came that characteristic roar which low-pressure tyres make as they pass over stone-paved roadway. We lurched through several sharp bends, then stopped. I heard someone climb out of the front seat and knock on a wooden door or gateway. There came the clatter and squeak of bolts being drawn. The car ran forward a few more yards, then came to a final halt. My two companions in the rear seat opened the door and handled me out. There was no point in resisting. Still blind, I was led, each of my arms firmly held, up a flight of steps, along a corridor and into a room.

The sack was pulled off my head.

'Sit down, Mr. Temple.'

The voice was dangerously polite, and I recognized it as Rostand's – the same voice I had heard at the Villa Negra. My eyes were gradually focusing to the light. I saw that I was in a small room furnished as a comfortable office and sitting-room. Schultz was seated at the desk. This time there was no false friendship on his face. His expression was one of undisguised hostility. Rostand was at the uncurtained window, which seemed to look directly out to sea. He was half standing, half sitting on the ledge. I thought he might be slightly drunk. He seemed excited and very full of confidence.

The third of the men waiting in the room was so small and insignificant that I had not noticed him till now. He sat hunched in the corner like a little wizened old mouse, watching the scene from huge saucer eyes.

'I hope you have had an enjoyable day, Mr. Temple, and not been too worried about your wife.'

'I've had a very interesting day,' I said. What I most needed was time. If Rostand was in the mood to banter so much the better. 'Mr. Zoltan Gupte and Mr. O'Halloran were both very hospitable.'

'O'Halloran!' Rostand exclaimed. 'But he was murdered last night.'

'Then you should really meet his ghost. It's just as good as the real thing. Even Gupte was taken in by it.'

Rostand glanced swiftly at Schultz and then back at me. 'You're lying. The police are looking for his murderer.'

'I'm sorry you don't believe me. I could have told you several other useful things.'

'Such as what?'

'For instance that you made a great mistake in killing Audry Bryce. That is what made the good Sam decide to turn Queen's Evidence – or Bey's Evidence, as I suppose they call it here.'

Schultz pushed his chair back and stood up.

'Let's cut out the fancy talking, Pierre.'

He turned towards me. His blue eyes with their curiously dead expression were absolutely merciless.

'I hope you have not been so unwise as to try any tricks. You have brought the glasses?'

'Yes. I have.'

'Then hand them over.'

'Not till I've seen my wife.'

Schultz sneered.

'You poor fool. Do you not realize you are now in our power? If you have the glasses it will be perfectly simple for us to take them from you.'

As two gorillas were still standing only a yard behind me this was demonstrably true. I took my handkerchief from my breast pocket, extracted the glasses and handed them to Schultz.

He opened them carefully and both he and Rostand bent their heads to scrutinize them.

'I hope for your sake these are genuine,' Schultz said. He looked towards the little man waiting fearfully in the corner. 'Come along, Armand. You can get to work now.'

Armand stooped to pick up the black wooden box at his feet. Schultz nodded to my two guards.

'All right. You can put him in with the woman.'

Once again my arms were seized. I was hauled out through the same door and pushed along to the end of the passage. I had time to register the impression that I was already in a kind of basement. The door at the far end opened out on to a flight of stairs, which led farther downwards. At the bottom was a heavy door with a massive lock. One of my guards twisted the key and I was thrust forwards. Behind me I heard the door crash shut and the big key turn. The place was so gloomy that I did not dare to step forward until my eyes had grown accustomed to the darkness.

Then I heard a voice which I knew.

'Paul! Have they hurt you?'

I moved forward and almost crashed on to my face as I stumbled on a further two steps leading downwards. Steve

179

had run to meet me, and it was only by going into her arms that I avoided falling.

We stayed like that for a few moments.

Then I said: 'No. I'm all right. What's more important is, have they – have they done anything to you?'

'No. Apart from making me lie on the floor of a car with a smelly old bag over my head. My main problem has been boredom. I've been sitting here doing nothing since about midday.'

'Where did they pick you up? Somewhere in the Rue de Rome?'

'Yes. I fell for a very old trick. A man pulled up beside me in a car and said you'd had a bad accident and I was needed back at the hotel at once.'

'Oh, Steve! I thought you were too experienced to fall for that one.'

Steve laughed softly.

'So did I. But when it actually happened— Paul, what are you doing here? Did they kidnap you?'

My eyes were beginning to become accustomed to the gloom. There was a window high up in the wall, and some of the light of the stars was filtering through. The two thugs had not turned off the bulb on the stairway outside, and a bar of light shone through the half-inch gap at the bottom of the massive door.

'No. I came by invitation, as it were.'

'You mean you walked into this? I'm not going to pretend I'm not glad to see you, Paul, but – you haven't let them take the spectacles? I believe that's the only thing that prevents them from killing us.'

'No. The spectacles are where they'll never get them. I gave Schultz a false pair. It's only a question of time before they find out that I've tricked them. We may be in for a rather sticky time, Steve.'

Steve put her head against my arm and squeezed my biceps.

'I feel I can face it better now that you're here.'

'What sort of place is this we're in? Is there a light switch?'

'It's outside the door, I think. Doesn't the smell give you a clue?'

I peered round in the darkness. Sure enough there was a musty, vinous aroma in the air reminiscent of a pub. I could just make out the shapes of two huge wine barrels. I put a hand to the dark walls and felt the cold bottom ends of row upon row of bottles.

'It's the cellar. But isn't that the sky outside?'

'Yes. I think the house above us must be built on a cliff. I've been able to hear the sound of the sea below this window.'

'Any chance of escape that way?'

'I'm afraid not. It's barred and covered with wire mesh. There's a bench over there if you'd like to sit down.'

Steve led me towards the bare section of wall under the window.

I said: 'Pity we haven't a couple of glasses. We could at least celebrate our reunion.'

'There is a glass somewhere. I saw it during daylight. I think I can find it.'

Steve began to grope about on a shelf which I could hardly see. I cursed myself for not remembering to put my pencil torch in my pocket. Still, the thugs would probably have taken it. I had felt their expert hands running over my pockets soon after I'd been hauled into the car. My gold cigarette-case, my lighter and my wallet had all gone. Perquisites of the profession, presumably.

'Here we are,' Steve said. 'It's quite a big one.'

'Good. We can share it. Now did you notice whether there was any champagne?'

'No. I'm afraid it never occurred to me to make wassail. There must be champagne somewhere. It's all neatly labelled and marked with prices.'

'By Timothy, Steve! Why didn't I think of it before? We must be underneath the Trou du Diable, Schultz's restaurant in Sidi bou Saïd. It's about the right distance and that matches up with you hearing the sea.'

I had begun to make an exploration of the bottles in the wine racks, trying to recognize, by feel, the different types.

'I think you're right. Some very tantalizing smells of cooking have drifted through to me, and all I had was bread and cheese.'

I said with false cheerfulness.

'Here we are; struck lucky first time.'

Under my fingers I could feel the distinctively wired, bulbous cork of a champagne bottle. I loosened the wire and began to prize the cork out. It would do neither of us any harm to have our spirits lifted. We would probably need a good deal of Dutch courage before long. I wished I had remembered to mention Le Trou du Diable to Forbes. The chances of his finding us here were very remote.

The cork came out with a pop that sounded curiously like a shot from a silenced automatic. I held the bottle at an angle and poured some of the bubbling liquid into the glass. We drank each other's health, sitting close together on the narrow bench. I held my watch in the bar of light from the door. It was just two o'clock, about fifty minutes from the time I had received the telephone call. I was sure now that the call had been made from somewhere in Tunis, nowhere near our present whereabouts, and that even at this moment Sir Graham might be making an abortive raid on some empty hide-out.

Silence was bad medicine under these conditions.

'I've found out a good deal since we last met,' I said. 'In fact this has been an extremely eventful day.'

I told Steve about the long chain of events which had kept me busy since that morning. She cheered up considerably when she heard that Sir Graham Forbes had appeared on the scene, and listened eagerly when I recounted the story of the Melrose jewels.

'I remember reading about that. Did Sir Graham explain what the significance of the spectacles was?'

'I'm afraid that was one gap in the otherwise very full picture he painted for me. Luckily I was able to fill it in for him.'

'Paul! You mean you've known the answer all along? How unfair of you not to tell me!'

'I haven't known it all along, but I began to have an inkling when we were discussing things last night. I was able to confirm it this morning soon after I so unwisely left you.'

I stopped to pour a little champagne into the glass. It was a pretty good vintage; probably 1952, I thought, and possibly a Delbeck. I was looking forward to seeing the bottle in the light and confirming my diagnosis.

'Well, go on!' Steve nudged me impatiently.

'When the gang decided to split up it was Leather who had the responsibility of hiding the loot. He took it to some place out in the desert and buried it. He then made an exact trigonometrical calculation of the spot and converted it into a prescription for a pair of spectacles. When the prescription was made up he was able to destroy all the other evidence of the whereabouts of the jewels.'

'What an absolutely marvellous idea!' Steve breathed. 'It seems impossible that anyone could hit on such an inspiration. How on earth did you guess it?'

'It was a bit of luck, really. I'd been on the fringes of a solution, and then simply because an old optician was a little on the deaf side, I suddenly saw the light.'

'I think he almost deserved to get away with that – this man Leather, I mean.'

'Leather was a remarkable man. He was the welding force in that gang – or syndicate, to give them a more flattering name. After his death they were all at each other's throats, each man out for himself.'

'How many of them were there? Rostand, Schultz, Leyland?'

'No. Leyland did not belong to the original syndicate. That consisted of Leather, Rostand, Schultz, Zoltan Gupte – he was the fence who could dispose of the jewels – and a fifth person.'

'Someone we haven't met yet?'

'As a matter of fact we have, but I think I'd rather you didn't know who it is just at this moment.'

'Do I know his name?'

'You know the name very well. It's David Foster.'

'I see. So David Foster really does exist, after all.'

'In a way, yes.'

Steve took the glass from my hand, and after taking a drink was silent for some moments. I thought it could not be long now till the little old man in the study upstairs gave his verdict. It would then be obvious to Rostand and Schultz that the prescription for Forbes's spectacles did not make geographical sense.

'How did Judy Wincott get mixed up in all this?'

I automatically felt for a cigarette, and then remembered that I had lost my case.

'You know the old saying: *cherchez la femme*. In this case it should be amended to *cherchez les femmes*, because the women provide a key to the whole business.'

I broke off. A shadow had fallen across the bottom of the door and there was a sound of feet descending the stairs.

'Keep your chin up, Steve,' I said. 'This is it.'

The key clattered in the lock and the door was flung open. Looming hugely in the doorway were the two thugs who had brought me there. Beyond them at the top of the flight of steps was Schultz.

'Bring them up!' he shouted harshly. 'Be quick about it.'

'Come on, *salaud*,' the larger of the thugs grunted at me. 'Any funny tricks and the woman gets it in the stomach.'

With an automatic levelled at my back I went ahead up the stairs. Schultz had returned to the study. He and Rostand were standing there when we were hustled in, and I knew by their faces that the truth was out. Forbes's glasses lay on the white blotter of the desk. The frightened little old mouse man had disappeared. Rostand had that unnerving, excited look on his face which I had seen before in the Villa Negra. Schultz, on the other hand, had gone a livid grey. He was in the grip of an overwhelming rage.

Rostand rushed towards me the moment we were pushed through the doorway.

'Hold his arms!' he hissed to the guards. My arms were pinioned to my sides while Rostand drove his clenched fist repeatedly into my cheeks, my eyes and my mouth. I rocked my head back at each blow, but I could feel the blood trickling into my eye and taste it on my tongue. He stopped abruptly when he found that his own knuckles had begun to bleed.

'All right, Pierre,' I heard Schultz say. 'We haven't any more time for games.'

He had seized hold of Steve when she tried to rush forward and throw herself on Rostand. He had her arm twisted behind her, and was able to hold her with one hand. She did not cry out, but she had turned quite white.

'Mr. Temple,' Schultz said with dangerous politeness. 'You have wasted a lot of time. I beg of you not to delay any longer in telling the truth. We are going to find out where those spectacles are, you know.'

Still holding Steve easily with one hand, he brought her towards the table just in front of me. She was gasping with pain when he pinned her other hand palm upwards on the table.

'Pierre,' he suggested, 'you have your automatic?'

Pierre groped in his pockets and produced a Beretta. He was watching Schultz for his cue.

'You know that a shot through the hand is one of the most painful wounds? I am going to count five and then Pierre will pull the trigger. One . . . two . . .'

Schultz, as I knew well, was not lying when he said that a hand wound is one of the most painful. I could feel the sweat breaking out all over my body. The hands that held me had tightened their grip.

'. . . three . . . four . . .'

'All right,' I said. 'I'll tell you. They're in the vaults of Lloyds Bank in Tunis.'

'How do we know you're telling the truth?'

'The receipt is in my wallet. One of your gorillas pinched it from me.'

The automatic was still aimed at Steve's hand. Schultz showed no surprise at my wallet having been stolen. He merely glanced up enquiringly and one of the guards, with a very sheepish look, produced it. Schultz released Steve's hand to flick it open. The money had vanished, but the small receipt from Lloyds Bank was still there.

'Let him go,' Schultz said, 'but keep him covered.' He addressed himself to me. 'Go to the desk and write on it: "Please hand the package specified on this receipt to the bearer" – then sign it.'

I went to the desk and wrote as he had directed. There was little doubt in my mind that I was signing both our death warrants, but I could never have steeled myself to watch Steve being shot through the hands. I handed the document back to Schultz. He and Rostand studied it.

'Will that do the trick?' Schultz asked the other man.

'Yes,' Rostand confirmed. 'They know me at Lloyds. There won't be any difficulty. It means waiting till to-morrow, that is all.'

'We can go to the yacht in the meantime. I think we've been here long enough, you know. The sooner we move the better.'

They were talking to each other as if Steve and I no longer existed.

Rostand said: 'Better make sure you haven't left anything important here.'

'I've checked all that,' Schultz said, casting a quick glance round the place.

Since he had relinquished his hold of Steve we were each of us watched by one of the guards, their automatics aimed suggestively at our stomachs.

'Let's go, then,' said Rostand. 'There's nothing more we can do here.'

Schultz turned to me as he stood at the door.

'I have enjoyed meeting you, Mr. Temple. Did I tell you that I have read one of your stories? I am so sorry I cannot provide you with a happy ending to this one.'

His voice changed as he addressed the two guards in French. 'I am leaving you to dispose of them. You know what to do.' The thugs nodded and the door closed on Schultz and Rostand.

'I suppose he means dump them in the sea,' the larger of the two guards said. 'Well, they may as well walk there on their own two feet as have us carry them. Come on, my friend. If you give us your co-operation we can make this nice and quick for you.'

I knew that Steve was looking towards me, but I dared not meet her eyes. I was feeling too ashamed of myself for not having the guts to suck it out or at least to make a fight for it before the odds against us became too heavy. Dimly in the background I heard the door of the house shutting. I imagined Schultz and Rostand climbing into the car.

Then abruptly a new sound came – the sharp unmistakable crack of a revolver followed by a brief and vicious burst from a sub-machine-gun. The two guards turned their noses towards the door like pointers.

I dived across the front of my own guard at the man who was covering Steve. I heard a shot go off as we both crashed to the ground. I think that desperation and fury must have given me a strength I'd never had before. I pulled the gunman's head back by the hair and banged it hard on the ground. His body went limp. I turned round to find out how Steve was faring. She was holding grimly on to the gun-arm of the other thug, her teeth gritted with effort. Her adversary had sunk on to one knee and was making only half-hearted efforts to resist her. Between us we soon had the automatic out of his grip. He immediately collapsed on the floor and grabbed for his right foot. The shoe was shattered and blood was spurting from it.

'What happened?'

'He shot himself in the foot when you dived across him.'

Outside the corridor a fusillade of shots sounded, followed by the sound of running feet. I could hear Schultz shouting as he came: 'Armand! Pierre! Open the windows. We will have to go down by the cliff.'

Two more shots were fired outside the door, and I heard a man scream with pain. Schultz wrenched the door open and came in dragging a wounded Rostand behind him. He locked it, and then turned to find himself looking up the spout of the two automatics which I held in either hand.

'Drop your gun,' I said, and fired one into the wood behind his ear just to show him that my aim was good. He dropped the gun.

'Now unlock the door.'

Schultz slowly did as he was told. Meanwhile out of the corner of my eye I saw Steve stoop and pick up his automatic.

'Now come and stand under that nice picture of Venice.'

With Teutonic dignity and the air of a man who knows how to face the firing squad, Schultz ranged himself against the wall under his aquatint of the Bridge of Sighs. Rostand had crumpled unconscious on the floor, his shoulder shattered by a bullet. The upward rolling eyes and drooling mouth showed that he was not shamming.

That was how the *Commissaire* Renouk and Sir Graham Forbes saw us when they kicked open the door.

Chapter Ten

'I STILL don't know how you tumbled to the fact that we were at the Trou du Diable, Sir Graham. You must have done some very rapid thinking.'

The three of us – Steve, Sir Graham and I – were sitting in room number three seven two, nursing hot cups of chocolate in our hands. The hotel had proved its reputation for round the clock service by sending up staff to change the mattress and bedding which had been stained by Leyland's blood. Our tentative request for hot chocolate had been seen to with smiling alacrity. Even a Hotel Matron had appeared to sponge my bruised face and put sticking plaster and lint over the cuts on my cheeks.

It was past four o'clock before we got back to the Hotel François Premier. We had seen Schultz hustled away by the none too gentle police, and watched while Rostand was loaded on to a stretcher and carried out to the ambulance. He died before reaching hospital. Both of the hired gunmen were in need of hospital treatment, one for a shattered foot and the other for severe concussion. They travelled in the same ambulance as the dying Rostand.

'I don't take much credit for finding you, Temple. The fact is that I was completely stumped. I tried to trace that telephone call. It had been made from one of the telephone booths on the ground floor of the hotel. So I was back to square one.'

Steve and I listened to Sir Graham with the cosy interest of children who know that the story is going to end up all right.

'So what did you do?' Steve enquired brightly.

'Well, I hadn't much to go on, and I was determined to recover my spectacles, you know.' Forbes broke off to give his low, rumbling laugh. 'So I raced round to the *Commissariat* and found Renouk. That took me about a quarter of an hour. I persuaded him that the only thing to do was raid every house marked on that map of yours. We were just going to give out the orders when this anonymous call came through.'

'Anonymous call?'

Steve and I laughed. We had both said the words in unison.

'Yes. This chap just phoned through to Renouk's office and stated baldly that if we were interested in the whereabouts of Mr. and Mrs. Temple we would do well to raid the premises known as Le Trou du Diable at Sidi bou Saïd. Then he rang off, and the rest you know.'

'Did he speak in English?'

Forbes nodded.

'Renouk took the call, but I heard him vainly trying to elicit the chap's name.'

'I think I can supply you with his name, Sir Graham.'

'Can you, Temple? Let's have it.'

'David Foster. He was as anxious as you were for his spectacles not to fall into the wrong hands.'

'Paul, I think you're being maddeningly secretive about all this,' Steve objected. 'Surely this case is all over now. Can't you tell me who David Foster is?'

'It's not over, you know. Only two members of the gang are in the bag. Three of them are still at large. They're just as desperate as Schultz and Rostand to get possession of those spectacles. And don't forget the unsolved murder of a friend of ours is still on our conscience.'

'You mean Judy Wincott? Paul, how does she come into all this?'

I swallowed the second half of my chocolate and felt it snaking down into my stomach and forming a comfortable, warm knot there. Sir Graham was leaning back in his armchair, breathing gently through his pipe and contemplating us both with the kindly affection of the Prodigal Son's father. Steve's colour had returned; she was very stimulated by the excitement and the sudden safety after danger. Her eyes sparkled and she found it hard to sit still.

I said: 'I think I'd just been telling you that the motto of this case should be *cherchez les femmes,* and that the women involved were the key to the whole business. You can correct me if I'm wrong, Sir Graham.'

Forbes nodded sleepily, content to let me do the talking.

'Even before he died, Leather's wife had deserted him for Rostand – which did not save her when she had outlived her usefulness. Leather's new girl-friend was one of a pair of dubious young ladies, who lived very well on their lawless boyfriends and were occasionally useful to them in their plans. Her name was Diana Simmonds, and her friend was called Judy Wincott. Now, when Leather was dying and semi-delirious, he confided his secret to Diana Simmonds, and bequeathed the spectacles to her. At first she could not quite believe in their immense value, but various disquieting incidents took place which warned her that there were people who would stop at nothing to gain possession of them. She became scared and confided in her friend.'

'This was all happening in Paris just about the time we were there?'

'Yes, and just a little before. Now Judy Wincott was the mistress of the second most powerful member of the syndicate – Webb. He suspected that Leather had given Diana Simmonds the spectacles. He did not dare to come into the open himself, but he offered Judy Wincott five thousand pounds to get the spectacles from Diana Simmonds and to send them to him in Tunis.'

'Then it was he who thought up the idea of using us as carriers?'

'He may have. On the other hand Judy Wincott was a pretty smart girl, and she may have hit on that plan herself . . .'

Steve had only been sitting in her chair for a few moments. Now she stood up and came to perch on the edge of the bed beside me.

'Then what happened on the night she came to the flat to give us the spectacles?'

I turned towards Forbes. 'That's your end of things, Sir Graham. Can you tell us what happened then?'

'Well, it's largely a matter of conjecture, Steve. We think that Simmonds followed Wincott to your flat, and while she was waiting downstairs was surprised and murdered in the belief that she had the spectacles.'

'Then what about Judy Wincott herself? How did she get to Nice and why was she murdered?'

'That's still an unsolved crime,' Forbes said. 'Mirabel is working on it, and I think he'll crack it in the end. You were very much under suspicion yourself at one time, Temple. Did you know that?'

'I was well aware of it, and it was a most uncomfortable feeling. I suppose it was you who told Mirabel that although

I had a way of attracting trouble I was not usually the prime cause of it?'

Forbes chuckled and struggled to his feet.

'I believe I did say something like that. Well, it's almost daylight, and I expect you two could do with some sleep.'

'I think we could.'

Steve and I both stood up as Forbes moved towards the door, stifling a yawn with the back of his hand.

'Sir Graham . . .' I began clumsily. 'It seems a rather flat way of saying it, but – thank you for what you've done.'

'Don't thank me,' Forbes replied cheerfully. 'Thank the anonymous caller. Good night, Temple. Good night, Steve.'

As the door closed Steve stood on her toes like a ballet dancer and stretched her hands in the air.

'I don't feel a bit like going to bed,' she announced. 'I'd like to go dancing or something.'

'It's the champagne. It's gone to your head. But I'm afraid we really ought to go to bed. We have a luncheon date to-morrow.'

'Oh? You didn't tell me that. Who with?'

'Tony Wyse and Simone Lalange.'

'Splendid! That'll be fun. They're the only two people we've met on this trip who haven't kept on nagging us about those blessed spectacles.'

'Yes, and as Sir Graham so rightly remarked, we ought to be very grateful to Mr. Wyse.'

'Oh, did Sir Graham say that? Why are we grateful to him?'

'Because he was the anonymous caller.'

The luncheon party the next day was a great success. Wyse was in excellent form, and repeatedly congratulated Steve on her escape from danger. Schooled by me she made no reference to the anonymous telephone call. We three drank cocktails in the American Bar until Simone Lalange turned up. Like most attractive women she was confident that her unpunctuality would be forgiven, and it was. Wyse insisted on standing another round of drinks. He was undoubtedly very struck by the French girl, and she played up to him unashamedly.

'We'd better go in to lunch,' I said after a time. 'Or everything will be eaten.'

I had reserved a corner table, and ordered a couple of different wines to be brought to the right temperature. We ordered our meal with great care. The occasion had very much the atmosphere of a celebration.

By the time we had eaten our first three courses the dining-room was almost empty. While the waiter was bringing the dessert Wyse reminded me that I had promised to show him the famous spectacles.

'Ah, yes. I almost forgot.'

Once again I removed my handkerchief and brought forth the pair of spectacles from my breast pocket. Simone Lalange was on my left, her enormous handbag occupying a large slice of table. I handed them to her first.

'You would hardly believe it, *mademoiselle,* but I have been offered as much as ten thousand pounds for these spectacles.'

'Ten thousand pounds!' she exclaimed. 'I think you are joking to me.'

'It's quite true.'

'I suppose they are magic spectacles, and when you look through them you see everyone is beautiful and handsome. May I see what Tony is looking like?'

She put them to her eyes, peering in mock seriousness at Wyse, who had sat on the opposite side of the table to her. She screwed up her eyes, shivering and hunching her shoulders.

'Ooh, it is like diving into the water! I do not think I can offer you ten thousand pounds, Mr. Temple.'

Wyse laughed appreciatively, and Simone handed the glasses to Steve.

'Would you like to try with them, Mrs. Temple? Perhaps you can make your husband even more a handsome man.'

She flickered her eye-lashes naughtily in my direction and I could sense Wyse bridling with jealousy.

'I use rose-tinted glasses when I want to look at Paul,' Steve said laughing. 'Would you like to have a try, Mr Wyse?'

She held out the glasses for Wyse. He was smiling at Simone as he took them from her, and not really watching what he was doing. The glasses clattered to the floor.

Wyse said: 'How clumsy of me!' He stooped and felt about under the table for a moment.

'No harm done,' he announced as he retrieved them. 'They're unbroken.'

He opened them up and examined them carefully.

'Well,' he said after a moment. 'I confess I'm a little disappointed. Personally I'd advise you to accept a fiver for these, Temple, if anyone makes you another offer.'

I took the glasses back and put them away in my breast pocket again. The waiter came with the dessert trolley, and we all broke off to choose what we would have.

Wyse had begun to drink more heartily, and by the time the coffee was before us he was in really high spirits.

'Do you take sugar, Mr. Wyse?' Steve asked him.

'Yes, please. And I do wish you'd stop calling me *Mr*.'

'What shall I call you then?'

'Why not try calling him David Foster?' I suggested.

Wyse's hands dropped to the edge of the table, and he became perfectly still.

'What the hell do you mean by that?'

'Would you prefer to be addressed as Webb, then?'

Still no movement from Wyse, just a curious hardening of his features. He suddenly looked quite different from the good-time boy we knew.

'I take it this is some kind of joke?'

'Not really. No more than your idea of getting us to bring the spectacles from Paris to Tunis for you. Or did Judy Wincott suggest that to you? It was a wise precaution. The Tunisian customs people seemed to be waiting for you, I noticed. They gave you a very thorough check over, didn't they? Perhaps they already had a description of Edmund Webb.'

'I don't know what you're talking about.'

Wyse had controlled his face and the couldn't-care-less expression was back. But he had forgotten his hands. They were clenching and unclenching on the white table-cloth. Simone Lalange's eyes had opened wide with amazement, and she was staring from one to the other of us with complete incomprehension.

'I think you do. I wouldn't really hold any of this against you, but for one thing. Steve and I are grateful to you for telephoning Renouk last night – though I know your motive was to prevent the spectacles falling into the hands of Rostand and Schultz. It's arguable that Constantin deserved to die, and I'm only sorry you did not hit that brute Sandros harder.'

Wyse ignored me and turned politely to Steve.

'Does your husband often indulge in these little flights of fancy?'

'What I can't forgive you for,' I went on, 'is killing your own friend, Judy Wincott. Why did you do that, Webb? Did she discover the true value of the spectacles and try to get a higher price for them than you were offering?'

197

Wyse's chair legs rasped harshly on the parquet floor as he pushed it back.

'I've enjoyed our lunch up till now,' he remarked with dignity, 'but I think this joke is becoming one-sided. If you will excuse me—'

'Hold on a second. You said you were disappointed with the spectacles, but I noticed that you took the chance of switching them for another pair under the table. You're going to be even more disappointed when you get home. That's a fake pair you've got. The real ones are now in the hands of *Commissaire* Renouk . . .'

Wyse's face gave a violent twitch.

'God damn you, Temple !' he shouted, and jerked upwards with his hands.

The table with all its glasses and cups went crashing on its side. Simone Lalange gave a scream and jumped to one side. Wyse was standing facing Steve and me across the table. He had pulled an automatic from his pocket.

'If anyone ever asked for this,' he grated, 'you did.'

I saw his hand begin to tighten on the trigger. The next instant the roar of a revolver crashed against our ear-drum. The automatic leapt from Wyse's hand and landed on the floor about ten feet away.

'No. Don't move,' Simone Lalange said.

With utter unbelief Wyse swung his eyes round to her. She was standing on firmly planted feet close to the wall and a safe distance away from him. A man-sized .38 revolver was rock-steady in her right hand, a wisp of smoke curling upwards from the barrel. It was a most incongruous sight – this beautifully turned out young woman with varnished finger-nails, false eye-lashes and immaculate hair, holding a lethal weapon with such undoubted assurance.

'What the—? Who—?'

Wyse could only stammer. He shook his head like a man who thinks he is dreaming.

'Meet *Mademoiselle* Carrière of Interpol,' I said. 'She's been on your track since Nice. But don't be too downhearted. She had me fooled for a long time too.'

Wyse took the useless glasses from his pocket and threw them among the debris of our lunch table.

'I should have known after that incident at the El Passaro Club. I suppose it was you who removed the spectacles from Temple's pocket and planted them in his wife's handbag?'

Simone smiled sweetly: 'I believe I remember something of the kind.'

'This is where I give up,' Wyse said with disgust. 'I think I've seen everything now.'

Three days later Steve and I were on the plane to Milan, from where we would pick up another flight direct to London. In the seat facing us was a gentleman of advanced age who had retained the unmistakable stamp of a military man. He studied us carefully during the journey, and listened with attention when we discussed what we would do when we arrived back in London.

We were losing height for the landing at Milan, when he leaned across the table and addressed himself to Steve.

'I hope you don't mind my speaking to you like this, but I couldn't help overhearing what you and your husband were saying. You are going on to London, I take it?'

'Yes, we are.'

The old gentleman reached into his travelling grip and brought out a square, flat parcel.

'I wonder if I might ask you to do me a very small favour? I have to spend several days in Milan, and I am most anxious that this should reach my little granddaughter for her birthday. It's to-morrow, and I really don't trust the post.'

Steve glanced at me, but I kept my head well down in my own book.

'I don't think I can do that,' Steve said firmly. 'My husband and I are both very particular about observing customs regulations.'

'But it's only a book!' exclaimed the military gentleman. 'I'll unwrap it and show you.'

He untied the knot and removed the paper. Then he held it up for Steve to see.

'It's only a copy *of Alice in Wonderland.* You can't say that's contraband.'

'I'm sorry,' Steve said definitely. 'I can't do it. We once knew some people who got into quite serious trouble through taking a package like that through the customs.'

The old gentleman's sniff showed clearly what he thought of us.

'Well!' he muttered as he wrapped the book up again. 'Young people these days don't seem prepared to raise a finger to help others.'